TAMA-RE

BOOK III

CHAOS To Order

TAMA-RE

BOOK III

CHAOS TO Order

Dr. Michael Berkley 33°

Berk Entertainment

Book three of the Tama-Re series.

Printed in the United States of America

ISBN: 978-1-956174-19-9

First Printing, 2022

Chaos

-Begins-

CHAPTER 1

A Nubian man lays in a circle. His head is pointing east, feet are pointing west, his left arm with its index finger extended is pointing south, and his right arm with its index finger extended is pointing north.

A man hovers over the Nubian man. He is standing on the letter "E" which is outside the circle. He wears an indigo cloak with the hood over his head. Another three men dressed in white cloaks stand to his left, then a man dressed in a blue cloak stands on the letter "S." Three more men wearing white cloaks stand next to him. A man dressed in a red cloak stands on the letter "W." Three men stand to the left of him, wearing white cloaks. Next to them is a man standing on the letter "N," wearing a yellow cloak and to his left are three men wearing white cloaks.

Twelve men, in all, stand outside of the circle, as the Nubian man paralyzed, lay helplessly in the center, looking like he is laying on an altar, as the ritual continues.

The man wearing the indigo cloak says, "Hail unto thee, who are Ra in thy rising, even unto thee who art Ra in thy strength, who travelest over the heavens in thy bark at the uprising of the sun. Aaron standeth in his splendor at the prow, and Ra-Har abideth at the helm. Hail unto thee from the abodes of night!

All the men respond, "Amen!"

Then the man wearing the blue cloak states, "Hail unto thee who art Hathor in thy triumph, even unto thee who art Hathor in thy beauty, who travelest over the heavens in thy bark at the mid-day of the sun. Aaron standeth in his splendor at the prow, and Ra-Har abideth at the helm. Hail unto thee from the abodes of the morning!"

The men respond two times, "Amen, Amen!"

The man wearing the red cloak adds, "Hail unto thee who art Atum in thy setting, even unto the who art Atum in thy joy, who travelest over the heavens in thy bark at the setting of the sun. Aaron standeth in his splendor at the prow, and Ra-Har abideth at the helm. Hail unto thee from the abodes of the day!"

The men say three times, "Amen, Amen, Amen!"

The man in the yellow cloak responds, "Hail unto thee who art Kephra in thy hiding, even unto the who art Kephra in thy silence, who travelest over the heavens in thy bark at the midnight hour of the sun. Aaron standeth in his splendor at the prow, and Ra-Har abideth at the helm. Hail unto thee from the abodes of the evening!"

The men hum, "Ommmmmmmmm."

The Nubian man is raised off the ground as the circle surrounds him. The circle begins to spin, while the Nubian man's body remains stationary in the center.

The men begin their procession, marching around the room, singing joyous hymns with great passion. Completing 7 circles around the room, they divide into four groups. Each taking a position in a corner of the room. Then the man in the purple robe gives a signal.

They all move simultaneously to the center, close to the Nubian man. His soul is seen leaving his body. Now, the Nubian man's body is lifeless.

"We have sacrificed the soul to Aaron. The lifeless temple awaits the great arrival of Aaron, who the creative force has appointed to sustain and end the world. We pledge our lives to him from who we receive them. Let us invoke his blessing."

The men raise their arms towards the lifeless Nubian and solemnly repeat, "we pledge our lives to Aaron, to him from who they came." Then they lower their arms, singing an anthem in which the Sacred Name was repeated many times, much as it is in the Aaron Chorus. The happiness and passion of the men is indescribable.

On 6-6-2019, the sacrifice occurred as the attempt to bring forth the one who the Aaronites believed wears the crown of the Magi.

***

"I want to thank you Jacob, for giving up Chosen." George Gardner gestures for Jacob to take a seat.

"You know the old saying, the enemy of my enemy is my friend," chuckles Jacob. "But we go way back Double G."

"Be honest with me, why did you give a brother of your order up?"

"He challenged me for my Sovereign Grand Priest position. He started telling the members that he had inside info to the Order of Aaron."

George looks upset.

"I knew he was lying, but the brotherhood began to believe him. They even wanted to add some of the rituals of Aaron to our order," says Jacob, sounding disgusted. "I knew this would bring problems to our order that we didn't want."

George replies, "you're an intelligent upright man. When we heard this outrageous claim, we began the plans on how to destroy your order." George looks towards the ground, "it's business, not personal."

"I see it as personal and business. I can't see how you would separate the two."

"Well, the so-called Chosen One is no more, we dropped his body off in a safe place. He will be met by the pigs."

Jacob knows not to mess with the Aaronites. If law enforcement uncovers Chosen's murder, they would make the case disappear like an unsolved mystery.

"By the way, he wasn't the Chosen One."

"Why do you say that?"

"Because the spirit of Aaron refused to take over his body."

Jacob looks in horror. He wonders what George means. What did the Aaronites do?

***

Jacob lays on his hospice death bed, explaining to Cue his part in the ritual that occurred on 6-6-2019.

"Do you regret what you did, elder?"

"Not at all. I did my part, my purpose. What I believed was best for humanity," Jacob confidently responds.

"But why the Aaronites?"

"I knew they were bold enough to begin the transition into the Age of Aquarius."

"The members of your order didn't have the same enthusiasm?"

Jacob says one name, "Dr. Freeman."

Cue laughs in a disrespectful manner, "I guess you're right. I still despise the thought of him. But you said the soul of Aaron didn't enter Chosen's body, so what happened to the soul that they called to earth?"

"Since the ritual failed and the energy was released into the physical realm, we have witnessed scenarios like the one that recently occurred where the police officer got into a physical confrontation with a black man over some presumed stolen items. The officer tased him, but it didn't affect him. He walked towards his car, looking at the video, I must admit that it looked like the man was hoping to avoid further confrontation.

The officer in pursuit, pulled out his .40 caliber Glock, demanding him to stop.

He continued to walk towards his car, as if, he didn't hear the command.

The officer shot him in the back 3 times, turns, and looks away, then looks at his hand as if in disbelief, shooting 4 more times, 7 in all.

The bystanders erupted in chaos because of another, police shooting. The masses are totally unaware that the soul of Aaron is taking over people's bodies to create chaos."

CHAPTER 2

It is a strange night. While a storm embraces the city, the sky looks to be a dark purple. Lightning streaks across the sky, forming bright white and yellow lines, reminding those who know the ancient sciences about the energy grid ley lines which cross the earth.

A dark cloud sits over The House of Africology. As Mischel, Robert, and Nathan stand in the basement, forming a triangular shape.

Nathan is wearing a black and red robe. He has a red tarboosh on his head. "I stand as TA, Earth's Physical Manifestation."

Mischel's hair is covered with a purple wrap. She is wearing a black and purple robe. "I stand as Ma, the Water that is energy in motion."

Robert is wearing a green and gold robe, with a black fez. "And I stand as Re, the light of the universe, sharing knowledge with those found worthy. Are you willing to take the oath of our great order? If so, say I am."

Dr. and Mrs. Thomas, Abraham, and Faith Cross simultaneously reply, "I am."

"Then you will kneel and repeat after us," explains Robert.

They kneel before Robert, Mischel, and Nathan who each says a part.

Once the oath has been repeated, Nathan says, "stand."

They stand.

Mischel replies, "you have now gained knowledge of the ancient land of Tama-Re which some call Egypt, and others call the entire continent of Africa. Continue to seek knowledge and go in peace."

The 4 new initiates are now members. The ceremony is over.

***

Earlier that morning, Robert and Mischel went to Lake Michigan for a morning stroll.

While walking, Robert suggests, "let's go to the Royal Star of the Lion site and work are way back."

Mischel replies, "let's do it."

They walk to the Royal Star of the Lion site. They both stand in silence as they look at its shape.

Mischel asks, "what now?"

"Say a prayer or affirmation, silently or aloud and walk with me."

Mischel nods to follow Robert's lead.

Robert walks to the center of the circle which has several lines crossing each other. He wonders if they are perfectly aligned with other sections of the city. He begins to pray out loud. "Infinite intelligence, thank you for guiding Dr. Freeman to us. We are now willing vessels, here to complete your purpose."

Mischel doesn't say a word. She intently listens, wondering where Robert received his words.

Robert continues, "As we turn to our left, we recognize that we stand as initiates and students of life."

They look in the distance.

Robert points at the two skyscrapers. "They remind me of pillars."

In between the skyscrapers, they recognize two pyramid shapes on top of two different buildings.

Mischel asks, "are those pyramids?"

Robert replies, "looks like." He pauses before continuing with his prayer. "We will use the power of the number 23, which you have shown those who walked before us, its perfect use." Robert turns to leave the circle.

Mischel follows him. "What do you mean by the number 23."

Robert stops and begins to explain, "the person influenced by the number 23 is fortunate. The number has a karmic reward. It promises success in one's personal endeavors, including one's career. A person with this number can possibly do great in business, if the individual uses the frequency which comes with the number. It pulls energy to assist and protect a person with this number from the higher spiritual realms. The number 23 offers permanent success, money, and fame throughout life. This number gives a person the power to defeat their opponent with ease. It also represents the widow's son because the number 2 is the mother, and the number 3 is the child. The number 1 is missing, which represents the father. Words like lion and king equal 23. It's very important to pay attention to words, as they hold specific vibrations."

"Your wealth of knowledge amazes me."

Robert walks to the bridge. He begins to walk up the stairs. As he walks, he counts each stair. "Infinite Intelligence, we have climbed 14 stairs. We recognize this as the foundation of our potential power." He walks across the bridge and down, counting 15 stairs. "Infinite Intelligence, we align ourselves with the power of Saturn and Christ Consciousness."

Mischel still listening, interrupts Robert. "Where did you learn all this?"

"It just came to mind."

Mischel looks and shrugs her shoulders. She is well aware that they are being influenced by higher vibrating energy forces. She grabs Robert's hand as they make their way to the next site. "Lead the way, love."

Robert smiles.

They get to the next site. Robert stops directly in the middle. He points to the box which seems to align perfectly to the middle.

Mischel nods.

"Infinite Intelligence, thank you for showing us the window to the soul of Milwaukee, as we stand at this, the Royal Star of the Bull site and the number 37," Robert affirms.

They walk to the curved brick wall.

Robert continues, "we recognize the horns of the bull and know to get to the next cycle the bull must be sacrificed. Yet, the horns represent the two extremes of a pole. So, we monitor the energy between intuition and reasoning and the spiritual realm and physical world. We turn to the apartment complexes behind us."

They are standing between two apartments, once again looking like pillars.

"We stand, again, as initiates and students of life, as the pillars are in front of us, and the pyramids are at a 90-degree angle to our left. Thank you, Infinite Intelligence for your continued trust in us."

Mischel kisses Robert, grabbing his hand tightly. She asks, "the number 37, please explain."

"Milwaukee equals 37. The number 37 represents spiritual power, leadership, fortune, and fame. The number 7 is the unseen or seen mysteries, and the number 3 represents creativity. This is a number good for making millionaires and developing great romantic relationships. As with the number 23, the number 3 represents the child. In this case, the child is encountering the mysteries of the universe." Robert looks at Mischel to make sure she is satisfied with his answer.

She nods, and they begin to walk to the next site. They stand at its entrance.

Robert begins by saying, "thank you Infinite Intelligence, we recognize life is a journey. We enter this ankh and reflect on the Royal Star of the man with the number 51."

They begin to walk forward.

"There are four pillars. Two on each side. We recognize the struggle we will encounter with our devotion between the creative force and humans. Yet, we remember that Infinite Intelligence has provided our individual foundations."

They cross the sidewalk to the second part of the structure.

"We are at the science of the number 7. We see the three pillars on our right."

Mischel looks at them.

Robert begins to explain, "the first pillar represents Grammar, which is the basic knowledge. The second pillar represents logic, as we gain a clear understanding. And the third pillar represents rhetoric, as we not only get a clear understanding, but we are able to utilize it to fulfill our purpose as it is laid out by Infinite Intelligence."

Before they enter the circle, they stop. Robert points at the two small pillars at its entrance.

Mischel nods again to confirm that she recognizes them.

"Infinite Intelligence, we enter the circle of power. You have guided the human mind to align the word circle with the number 32. We feel the power, within the circle."

Mischel interrupts, "we sure do." She holds on tight to Robert as if she is scared.

Robert smiles, kissing her on her forehead to let her know everything is alright. "We walk around the circle in the middle. We recognize it as the letter "O," which is the 15th letter in the alphabet. The American flag is on a pole which stands in the middle. The word America like circle, power, and Christ equals 32. We now leave the circle full of energy."

They walk back down the sidewalk.

"To our right, we arrive at the first pillar which represents arithmetic or numerology. Everything can be translated with numbers. The next pillar represents Geometry. The physical symbols which are the slowing of energy to manifestation. The third pillar is music or the vibration. It is the energy force between the physical and the spiritual, as we need it to flow up and down, back and forth from the lower to the higher realm. The fourth pillar is astronomy or the heavenly bodies. It also represents the spiritual world. We must remember how they affect us and utilize them for our benefit."

They walk back to the beginning section.

"Infinite Intelligence, we are grateful for the reminder that you are our foundation." This time Robert grabs Mischel's hand. He begins to explain, "this structure is the number 51. It is the reverse reflection of the number 15. Yet, the number 51 is one of the most powerful numbers in the 6 series, since 5+1=6. People who vibrate with this powerful number started from a humble origin and can possibly advance to an unimaginable height. Since they possess an abundance of energy, they can work very long hours without a lot of sleep, progressing to their goals quickly. It's a number that holds the vibration to many privileges. It indicates the perfect from rags to riches story. These people are also gifted with physical and psychic strength."

They leave the Royal Star of the Man site, walking to the last site. Robert mentions, "this sort of reminds me of the temple of Luxor." He shrugs his shoulders. He hasn't paid much attention to the last site. Because of this, he knows the energy force must flow through him to properly understand its message.

They walk in the square next to the site.

Mischel comments, "the queen sits her chosen king on the square."

"And the chosen king must remember to stand squarely on the square," adds Robert.

They walk to the entrance. Robert points at the two pillars.

Again, Mischel nods.

"Ready?"

Mischel nods again.

Robert says, "Infinite Intelligence, thank you for your guidance."

They enter the pillars.

Robert is guided to walk along the grass. "We walk beside the length of the grass. It is the measurement of 4x4 or 16 of the Pythagorean Theorem triangle. Pythagoras is the Egyptian Deity Ptah, who is reminding us of our current foundation.

We turn to the right along the grass representing manifestation. It is 5x5 or 25. We arrive at the 3 pillars and stand at the second pillar. We bow to Infinite Intelligence, seeing the compass on the ground which represents the Royal Star of the Earth.

We raise our heads, standing in the Southeast corner, looking towards the northwest. We see the hidden symbolism with the lighthouse. It is a staff, meaning the old man, who has studied and mastered geometry, leans on his staff for support.

Infinite Intelligence, you are truly amazing. You've guided humans to consciously, even subconsciously, place the sciences in a perfect position. We walk and recognize that nothing stays the same. We will have new foundations with the four pillars on our left, representing the mother, and on our right is the grass representing the father, but this time he stands as the number 3 of the Pythagorean triangle. We leave the 4 pillars onto the 5 pillars, having no meaning across from it, which shows us that there is more to be manifested."

Robert and Mischel get to the end. They look across the street to the mansions on the hill.

Mischel replies, "wealth."

Robert looks and hugs her. "Abundance," and then they kiss.

"But Robert, you didn't mention what number this site aligns with."

"This is the number 65, 6+5=11. The number 11 shows a person with the gift of visualization. This person can see what others can't in the past, present, or future. This number is the opening to a spiritual gate way, which is why the two number ones resemble pillars. Pillars are what initiates walk through in some ceremonies. A person with the number 65 has favor with the government. It's a karmic number with great recognitional rewards. It has a protective force, acquiring monetary gains by serving others. This number is a seeker of justice. It pulls energy from Mercury, the moon, and Venus. It has the power to present wealth and stardom. People with this number have a beautiful physique but are prone to danger and accidents."

***

When they arrived back to The House of Africology, Mischel goes to her study.

Time passes as the sisters of Huda fade away. Mischel gets up from her seat. She walks back into the living room where Robert waits.

"So?" Robert impatiently asks.

"Well..." Mischel giggles and has a long pause.

"Oh, this is funny to you," Robert showing even more that he is extremely anxious.

Mischel laughs even louder.

"Um I'm waiting."

"Okay, Okay, the Sisters of Huda said..." Mischel pauses again and looks at Robert as he fidgets.

Robert sits shaking his head, "if I didn't love you so much, I would get up and walk away."

Mischel smiles, still giggling, "they said that I've advanced passed the master number 55 and am well prepared to obtain the lessons of the master number 88."

"So, you should add Turner to Ziad instead of getting rid of the name Ziad?"

"Yes, making my new name Mischel Ziad-Turner."

Robert gets up and picks Mischel off the ground, hugging her, while kissing her all over her face. When he puts her down, they walk to speak to Nathan.

Nathan is sitting at a desk writing.

Robert asks, "what are you doing now Elder?"

"Playing with numbers." Nathan walks to the whiteboard. "Look at this, multiplying a number by itself, adding the next odd number in a sequence, starting with the number 3, then 5, 7, etcetra. There is an interesting pattern." Nathan begins to write on the whiteboard.

$$1 \times 1 = 1\ldots\ 1 + (3) = 4$$

$$2 \times 2 = 4\ldots\ 4 + (5) = 9$$

$$3 \times 3 = 9\ldots\ 9 + (7) = 16$$

$$4 \times 4 = 16\ldots\ 16 + (9) = 25$$

$$5 \times 5 = 25\ldots\ 25 + (11) = 36$$

$$6 \times 6 = 36\ldots\ 36 + (13) = 49$$

7x7=49.... 49+(15)=64

8x8=64... 64+(17)=81

9x9=81... 81+(19)=100

10x10=100. And so on."

"There are number patterns everywhere I see. The number 3 being the first odd number and the number 5 being the second odd number also aligns with the number being multiplied by itself," Mischel responds.

Nathan states, "good eye, I didn't see that."

"Oh, I see you have a picture of Benjamin Franklin and his kite again," implies Robert.

Nathan answers, "the brazen serpent."

"What's that?"

"The kite is 4 infinite triangles in 1, forming a diamond shape, better yet a divine tetragram. The rope represents the serpent, and the lightening represents the boldness."

"Wow, you didn't tell me that before."

Nathan says, "oh ok," shrugging his shoulders.

Mischel changes the subject. "Well, the Sisters approved that my name shall be Mischel Ziad-Turner."

"Ah so you are adding 33 to your personality number, making your new number 88."

"Yes, but can you tell me a little more?"

Nathan smiles and erases the whiteboard. He writes the number 55, first. "The number 55 represents the master of innovation. The number equates to freedom, success, wittiness, and a new path creator. This is why it made sense that you would be the perfect person to be the face of The House of Africology."

The logo for The House of Africology has an outline of Mischel's face.

Mischel smiles in delight.

Nathan continues as he writes 5+5=10 on the whiteboard. "In the way we use numerology, the two 5s are added together, equaling 10. This number is the wheel of fortune and shows us that the individual has infinite potential because of the divinity of the zero. In our order, we recognize that this person has passed the first level of 9 and is qualified to be initiated to the next level."

Robert inquires, "a higher level?"

Nathan responds, "a higher level depends on the person. So, we simply say a different level."

"Interesting."

Then Nathan writes 1+0=1 on the whiteboard. "Leaving the compound number, we reduce the 10 to the natural number 1. A number 1 person is comfortable at being self-sufficient. This person is a leader but has to be careful because she can also be too giving or too selfish."

"Too giving is my issue," as she reflects on how Stacey gave her idea to Cue's family, who has been capitalizing from it.

"When a person changes the name without mastering the birth numbers, the person can be extremely out of alignment because they are receiving an entirely new energy flow. We usually see this with women who get married. Their whole energy pattern shifts, and they don't know why.

Mischel, you have obviously proven to the realm of the angels that you are prepared to transition to another energy pattern. You will still be affected by the numbers 55, 10, and 1, but now you will experience the powerful number 88.

88 is the master of knowledge in the material world and beyond. You will experience a flow of energy like true scientific analysts feel. You will be highly intuitive and have an interest in business and acquisitions dealing with wealth. It's a number that deals with assertiveness, universal laws, authority, eternity, and self-discipline on a higher level. It is also the number of pioneering."

"She seems to be aligned with the plans of the future," Robert inquisitively inquires.

"Exactly, let's continue to see more, because I think she has been advanced to the sisterhood of Seshat." Nathan writes 8+8=16 on the whiteboard. "The number 88 reduced, equals 16. The number 16 represents the creator working with the human consciousness equivalent to Christ or Christ-consciousness. The number 15 equals Christ-Consciousness and Saturn. Therefore, the number 16 represents that the lessons of the mysteries of Saturn or Christ-consciousness have been completed." Again, Nathan writes on the whiteboard, this time he writes 1+6=7. "The number 16 reduced to its natural number is the number 7. As you know, the number 7 represents physical perfection.

Looking back at the double 8s, it is a very karmic number because of one 8, but you have two 8s. What you do, either positive or negative will come back to you very quickly. Thus, you must be cautious of your thoughts. You should really study this 88. You will see it used throughout different occult practices."

"I definitely will, Nathan, thank you," Mischel replies with much gratitude.

"When are you leaving for Egypt?"

"We are leaving in a few weeks. I'm just glad we can now sign the paperwork, since we've been married since February 22nd."

Mischel adds, "Don't forget the year, 2022."

"All those 2s, you are definitely either a couple made in heaven or destine for battle against each other."

"We'll take the heaven and battle against others not ourselves, thank you," Mischel sarcastically replies to Nathan.

Nathan laughs, "you are one of a kind Mrs. Ziad-Turner."

Mischel laughing, gets up, and leaves Nathan and Robert in the office.

***

Nathan set up his new office in The House of Africology. It had much less room compared to his other office, yet he still showed his exquisite taste. The office walls are painted black with diamond layered golden tiles on the side walls.

Two golden display cabinets with different golden ornaments and lighting stand to the left of his desk. The desk is a black glass mounted on a golden six-sided stretched polygon shape with a golden layer in the middle. The shape looks like the line of two arrows. He has four black chairs around his desk.

Behind his desk is a wall with white and black marble tiles. He has a black cabinet with designs on the doors, outlining the same shape as the bottom of his desk. Above the cabinet are two mirrors outlined in gold trim.

Robert says to Nathan, "it would have been nice if you could join us in Egypt."

"I would have loved to travel back to Egypt, but we just secured the 19 acres in the 30th Street Corridor area. I must finish the paperwork. I definitely don't want to lose it because of some mishap."

"I understand," Robert replies. "I was thinking that it would be kind of interesting to build some pyramids in the 30th Street Corridor area like those in Egypt, but we would make them black instead of brown."

"That would be interesting. The Grand Master would sometimes say 'we should bring Egypt to America, since so many of the family members live here.' 30 is also an excellent number because it represents infinite creativity. We can create that village that so many claim is needed to raise a child."

Robert doesn't say a word. He begins visualizing what the 19 acres could possibly look like.

Abraham walks into the office, overhearing the idea of the black pyramids. "It would be nice to put these new solar panel sidings on the pyramids, if they are built on the property. We could make them black like the glass on your desk, Elder Nathan."

"So, you have something new, Ab?" Robert curiously asks as he snaps out of his thought.

"Yes, I have an advance class at the Midtown building. We are working on a large solar panel project. I think we can adjust them to be very large sidings for the pyramid."

"That would generate a lot of needed energy, reducing our utility bills," says Nathan.

"We could harness more energy from the pyramids like they did in Egypt."

Robert asks, "you've studied the pyramids over there, Ab?"

"Most scientists, engineers, and programmers that I know have been curious of the pyramids in Giza. Some say that they were used for healing. One story claim that there used to be water that floated around the base. Individuals would place their heads in certain areas. The sound generated from the running water would heal them like tuning forks heal people today."

"Wow, I have to keep that in mind when I'm over there. Nathan are you still thinking about a shipping container city?"

"Yes, but there's some new technology in Mexico where they shoot cement in specially made material. This may be better and longer lasting. Everything depends on the city's policies. I'm still studying the possibilities, so, we will see."

***

Robert and Mischel go to bed.

Robert begins to dose off. His eyes begin to roll back in his head. He has learned this is the starting point of him receiving a visit from the spiritual realm. Time passes and he hears.

"Robert, when you go to Egypt, you are to find the black man wearing the red collar."

Robert responds, "Dr. Freeman, it is good seeing you again."

Dr. Freeman gives the sign of Huda.

"Is this man a part of Huda?" Robert asks.

"You have been given all the tools to recognize if he is a part of our great order or not. You must use them to answer your question."

"But if he isn't in the brotherhood, what am I supposed to gain from him?"

"Time will tell. The key is to be open minded and patient. Use the tools to work on yourself as well." Dr. Freeman leaves.

Robert pulls himself out of the vision state. He rushes to grab a pen and paper. He didn't place them by his bed this shadow but knew the importance of writing things down. He writes the message. He has learned from the horrific feeling he gets, when he forgets the message because he didn't write it down.

CHAPTER 3

Although Mischel and Robert were scheduled to leave for Egypt in the morning, Nathan wants Robert to accompany Abraham, Dr. Thomas, and him to Milwaukee City Hall. Lead politicians, including Mayor Chanokh, are listening to companies, attempting to win the city contract for the demolition of old buildings around the city.

They get to City Hall before everything begins. Nathan makes sure that he is one of the first people at events like this. He wants to see the interaction between the people. He especially wants to see which politicians are working together or at odds. It all shows with their body language.

The room is filling up slowly.

Nathan says to the brothers, "I don't think people will pack the room."

They continue to sit and wait. Nathan gets up to walk out. He motions Robert to follow him. They don't say a word to each other. They stand watching as the alderpersons and mayor arrive.

The alderpersons greet Nathan as they walk in. Robert knows that Nathan is a popular individual. Then Mayor Chanokh walks up. He greets both Nathan and Robert, rushing into the room as if he's late.

As Nathan predicted, the room isn't fully packed. Facing the attendees, the 6 alderpersons and the mayor sit in a semi-circle in the front of the room. The audience is separated from them by a table, where the presenters will sit, and behind the table is a small wooden gate like in a courtroom.

The president of the committee, holding a gavel, opens the meeting in a ceremonial fashion similar to those of secret societies. During the ceremony, they say the pledge of allegiance to the flag. Then the president gives the instructions and calls the first presenter. The presenter opens with several stats of the city. He explains what his company does and will do. He throws some more numbers out, then closes his presentation. His presentation was very dry.

The next presenter is called up. He does a similar presentation. His slides are much more colorful. But his head is down as he reads his notes.

Nathan nudges Robert to look at Mayor Chanokh. Robert gets Abraham and Dr. Thomas' attention. The mayor's attention is off in the distance somewhere. He even seems to be doodling instead of taking notes. Even though the presentation was livelier, the mayor paid little attention to what was being said.

Two more groups present. The president closes the meeting.

***

"So, what do you think?" Nathan asks the brothers.

Robert immediately responds, "I hope we aren't getting into demolition?"

Nathan chuckles, "No."

"I'm glad."

Dr. Thomas says, "they could have done a lot better with their numbers. A true mathematician would have questioned their calculations."

"I think they should have done more research on the city's 20-year plan. All the companies were looking at, how can I say this?" Abraham pauses to think of the best words, "they were looking for the immediate gratification. I believe if they would have added more information about the future-plans, it may have kept the mayor's attention."

"Yeah, the mayor was totally out of it. It was like he was sketching his fingers, making those turkey pictures that we drew in kindergarten," Dr. Thomas jokingly adds.

The brothers laugh nearly uncontrollably.

Nathan was laughing so hard that he has to turn around to get his composure. When he turns back towards the brothers, he says, "the presenter definitely needed to watch his audience."

Robert curiously inquires, "what could he have done to get the mayor back focused?"

Nathan answers, "what he could have done was called the mayor out by name. This would have caused the mayor to have some internal embarrassment, depending on his emotional stability, the mayor may have openly shown his embarrassment or pushed his paper to the side to refocus on the presentation. It's all about human psychology."

"To me, it's as if a company was already chosen. They just had to go through the motions to make it seem like they were giving the community a chance," adds Abraham.

"Possibly," responds Nathan. "Robert let me let you go. You have a great adventure ahead of you, as a newly married man and your tours in Egypt."

Robert replies, "thank you. Yeah, I should be leaving. You know my wife doesn't play."

The brothers laugh. They give departing words and leave.

***

Robert calls Mischel on his way home. "Do you need me to pick anything up?"

"No, I think we have everything. I'm quite anxious. I can't wait to see Egypt. I got in contact with an old friend. She told me about this tour in the Coptic Church. So, I made arrangements for our tour guide to take us there."

"That didn't affect our agenda, did it?"

"It did a little, but I was able to readjust things. We won't miss any of our other site tours."

"You're the best. Well, I'm on my way home."

"Walt"

"Yes ma'am."

"Do you remember the card I showed you with the juggler, the number 8, and the two 5-pointed stars?"

"Yes, you and this new tarot card thing."

"I was doing some research. It seems one of the meanings is the 5-pointed stars represent the sun in our galaxy and Sirius A in the Sirius binary star constellation."

"Seriously, Sirius A and Sirius B."

"Stop joking."

Robert laughs, "I couldn't let the opportunity slip. Anyway, sorry, please continue."

"Smart Aleck, supposedly Sirius A and Sirius B are like the parents to our sun. Their orbits cross at a specific time, looking at the orbits, a person may think of the number 8."

"Hold on let me pull over but continue."

"If this is the case, the tarot card illustrators have put some serious symbolism into these cards. The number 8 represents the constant movement of the star constellations. I don't know how many years they take to cross each other, but they obviously do."

While Mischel is talking, Robert pulls over his car. He pulls out a piece of paper and writes the name Moses. He writes the numbers equivalent to each letter (M=4, o=6, s=1, e=5, s=1). Then he adds the numbers, "Wow."

"What are you thinking?"

"Remember a few years ago when I told you the Moses story."

"A little."

"Let me attempt to refresh your memory. Moses went to get the tablets, but the people were impatient, having Aaron make a golden calf. The golden calf represented the golden era of Abraham or Taurus. They were in a time of a great reset, entering the Age of Aries."

"Oh yeah, I remember. You explained it as Egypt was the feminine/passive/still principle and Israel was the masculine/active/moving principle. The active can't do anything without the passive. But the Israelites felt they didn't need to hold on to the foundational information of Egypt or the slow-moving feminine energy, so, they went off to do their own thing, and they were messed up. This caused Moses to go into his higher mind, to retrieve the information he learnt in Egypt. He repackaged it and gave it in the form of the 10 commandments."

"I didn't say it like that, but you go baby. You are truly a teacher."

Mischel sarcastically responds, "I thought you already knew."

Robert sits in his car shaking his head. "You are hilarious. I do my best to keep up with your wittiness, but it's difficult." Robert pauses to get back on track with what he was thinking, "I wrote the name Moses down which equals 17 or 8, depending on how you calculate it. The tablets each had 5 commandments on it."

"The 5-pointed star," Mischel excitingly interrupts.

"Exactly, Moses is juggling between his devotion to God and his devotion to humans. A leader always is in a serious or should I say Sirius juggling act," Robert chuckles. "We should talk about your cards some more this shadow. I want to see if they align with the biblical stories. You have me interested."

CHAPTER 4

Jacob hands over the torch to Cue. Cue is now the Sovereign Grand Priest of The Africology House.

Jacob tells Cue that, "it's probably best that you change the entire name of The Africology House. Let it die with me, because Dr. Freeman's participation with it dies too."

"Are you sure?"

"Yes, plus I've given you all the information which I hold. Now I give you the rituals and by-laws of the higher degrees within our research order." Jacob points to a briefcase sitting in the corner of the room. "My wife brought it this morning. Now it's yours. Hold it close to you. It was passed to me by our prior Sovereign Grand Priest. He gave me the instructions to govern the order how I felt fit. I give you the same directions."

"Can I presume that the by-laws allow me to change the name of the order?"

"You are correct."

"What should I name it?"

"That's for you to decide. You have your own mind. Look at what we did before you and add your own ideas. We aren't a dictatorship. We are an ever-flowing order like the waves that ebb and flow on the shores of the ocean."

Cue sits for a while contemplating on his next moves.

An hour goes by, when Jacob announces, "my ancestors have come to me. It's that time for me to transition. I trust you are the right person to continue the mission." He waves Cue to his bedside.

Cue gets up and walks over to Jacob.

"This is the sacred handshake for our position. Let me whisper the sacred word into your ear."

Cue leans down to Jacob.

Jacob whispers the word.

Cue rises.

"Now my brother, I must ask you to leave. I will spend my final moments with my wife and children."

"Can I ask a question before I leave?"

"Please do."

"Why didn't you pass this information to your children?"

"This information isn't based on our direct biological lineage. We base it on the soul energy found within a person regardless, if they are immediate family members or not."

Cue nods his head to clarify that he understands. He bows giving the sign of respect to one who is departing. Then leaves the room. He passes Jacob's wife and children, giving his condolences and not telling them that Jacob will soon transition. Cue leaves the hospice building.

***

Later that day, Cue meets Chanokh to discuss his experience with Jacob. "He gave me the reigns to the order."

"You mean the Africology House?"

"Right, I'm now the Sovereign Grand Priest."

"Now what?"

"Although I would typically need you to be the next in charge, you're the mayor of the city. You hold several keys, even though we know who runs it." Cue adjusts himself in his seat. "What's even more interesting is Jacob let me know about a ritual the Aaronltes did. They released an energy which is wreaking havoc on the world."

Chanokh looks at Cue in shock.

"He also told me that several secret societies are doing rituals attempting to harness the same energy. They just don't realize that it has been released into the world."

"How did the Aaronites release it?"

"Jacob gave them the ancient Nubian ritual. They sacrificed a black man."

Chanokh gets very uncomfortable. He doesn't say a word as his body stiffens.

"As the mayor, I think it's good info for you. It gives you the answers to why things seem so out of control."

"Oh, you can believe I appreciate the information. In fact, while you were speaking, I was sitting here thinking of the interview that caused so much uproar which occurred March 7 at 8 PM Eastern time with Mary Blazel and her husband who is called bedevil in several circles. You know the man I'm speaking of, Anthony Henry Dye, the software programmer turned human health activist. It was strange. I wonder if that was a ritual too?"

"I have no clue."

***

Since Cue and Chanokh are both well respected men of the community, Jacob's family told them that Jacob requested they both be present at his viewing before the actual funeral. They were given special seating. Chanokh sits close to the aisle.

However, Jacob's casket isn't open. The casket is well decorated. It has all types of designs on it. There is also a picture of Jacob in his police uniform.

A few moments after they take their seats, a short medium build dark complexion lady with a short afro approaches Cue.

"Are you Cue?"

"Yes."

She hands him a pendant, "my uncle told me to give this to you."

Cue looks at the pendant, "thank you."

"He told me to tell you that only a queen can put a king on the throne." She walks away as fast as she arrived.

Chanokh looks at Cue, "I wonder what that was all about."

"It sounds like another ritual." Cue puts the pendant on.

Guests begin to arrive to view Jacob's body. People automatically recognize Chanokh and greet him by calling him, Mr. Mayor.

A few of the guests strangely bow to Cue as they pass.

When the funeral begins, Cue admires the colorful funeral program. He sees a picture of Jacob when he was younger, standing next to the billionaire Bob, Officer George Gardner, and several other men that he doesn't know. He realizes Jacob was deeply involved with some very powerful people.

After the service, Cue looks for his wives. When he finds them, he affectionately kisses his newly born sons. Diamond has his oldest son, and Ebony has his second oldest. He looks at the two boys as if they are in line to one day where the pendant he was just given. He knows Jacob told him that the leadership isn't necessarily given to a direct biological family member, but Cue plans on training his sons to sit on the throne.

Chanokh approaches Cue, "excuse me, sir."

Cue looks at him in a disturbed manner. "What is it?"

Chanokh leans forward and says in a low voice, "Bob has requested to see us."

Cue nods. He looks at his wives and says, "I have to attend to some business. I will see you at home." He turns and follows Chanokh to the minister of the church's office.

When they get in the office. George Gardner and Bob are waiting.

George welcomes Cue, "I didn't mean to get rough with you at your house. How are you?"

Cue looks at George with a disgusted demeaner and answers, "I'm well."

Bob adds, "George and I were discussing an issue that we have in the city."

George nods in agreement.

"There's a guy who is spreading a lot of conspiracies about our work and us."

"Can't you just send the detective here to rough him up like he did me and my family," responds Cue still upset wIth what George did at his house.

"It's not that easy this time," George declares.

"Are you saying what you did to my family and me was easy?"

"That's exactly what I'm saying," insists George.

Cue is filled with anger. He feels George sees him as weak.

Bob interrupts, "this guy is well connected in the black community. He has a great reputation and is the Grand Master of the craft."

"The craft?"

"Yes, he leads the Enlightened Masons in the state of Wisconsin. He has a large membership roster."

"I see." Cue looks at Bob and George very interested, wondering what is being said about them.

Chanokh sits not saying a word the entire time.

"What would you like me to do?" Cue asks.

"Just explain how it is important for him to change his rhetorical nonsense," replies Bob.

"If it doesn't work?"

George demands, "I will take matters in my own hands."

"That's exactly what I'm talking about. You should take this matter into your hands."

Bob in a calmer manner says, "Cue remember I told you when I needed you, I'd call upon you?"

"Yessir."

"Well, this is that time. We have made a deal to bring some new medical technology to the city that was created by Anthony Dye. We have the opportunity to be the first to get our hands on it, but this character is scaring black people with all that conspiracy theory nonsense."

CHAPTER 5

Chanokh sits with Nathan and Cue to get advice about law enforcement. They are meeting at Club Nefer, in Cue's office.

"What is your position on the police, elder?" Chanokh curiously asks the banker.

"Well, I do believe that we need them. I also believe as technology gets more sophisticated, so should they."

"You can't be saying give the police more funding," Cue interrupts, surprised at what Nathan is saying.

"That's exactly what I'm saying."

Cue barks, "but they have never helped us. They hate us."

"The word never is a broad statement. We have had incidents, but if you defund them, the less wealthy people will be more at risk."

Cue looks at Nathan in obvious disagreement. "What do you mean?"

"I look at things in a financial way. 80% of the population owns 20% of the wealth."

"Leaving 20% of the population owning 80% of the wealth, I get it, but..." adds Cue.

"Exactly, in other words, 80% of the population is struggling for a very small amount of the wealth. Without some type of governmental control, the struggle will get out of hand."

"People can be left on their own to figure things out."

"Listen Cue, we are in a capitalist society. People have taken what the Nubians who walked before us established, making it seem demonic. Yet, it gives an opportunity to create a heaven on earth, as long as the government doesn't overregulate things."

"So, you're saying Africans made the capitalist system."

"Yes, it was a group of Nubians who created the mercantile system, which was the beginning of capitalism. These Nubians were always outnumbered, so they had to constantly relocate. In the process of relocating, they hid their true intention. They were always 10 steps ahead of everyone."

"What do you mean, they hid their true intentions," responds Chanokh.

Nathan continues, "I'll give an example. They took the Geneva Bible and added cryptic codes."

Sipping his drink, Cue says, "I never heard of the Geneva Bible."

"Most haven't, after the cryptic coding was put in it, it was called the King James Version Bible."

"Wow," exclaims Cue. "Is this the type of research The Africology House was conducting."

"This is just one example. It's important to examine and reexamine Nubian history. We are more than slaves."

"I get that, but what can we do to stop police abusing us."

"First, they have to understand that this capitalist system was not set up like the communist system of a police state. Their job comes with a lot of authority and responsibility." Nathan pauses and looks directly at the Mayor. "Think about it Mr. Mayor. The city allows 21-year-old people to get hired on the police force and all they need is a high school diploma or GED. What did you know at 21, Cue?"

"Not much."

Still looking at the Mayor, Nathan continues, "It's been said that a person isn't an adult until the age of 40. So, you're giving these basically immature people a small window of training to make, in some cases, life or death decisions."

"That's a lot of power for a young person."

"Put on top of that, what if they feel black people are inferior to them?"

Chanokh states, "all signs of future police abuse."

"Therefore, I suggest looking at how they are being evaluated and trained. I think questions about race should be added to the lie detector test, if they don't exist. And another thing, black people are known to compete against each other. There will be another element of superior feelings among black officers."

"Something to think about," Chanokh says.

"Not only something to think about, but something to work on," insists Cue.

***

Cue calls Jazmine in the office, "could you please escort the elder to his car?"

"No problem."

Cue and Chanokh shake Nathan's hand. Then Nathan follows Jazmine.

Cue and Chanokh sit back down.

Cue responds, "he doesn't seem to know that I'm leading The Africology House now. We have to stop him."

"What do you mean?"

"We can't allow him to build up the land you got for him at the 30th Street Corridor site. If he is given that much power, he will make our move look like roaches."

"What do you suggest?" Chanokh asks.

"Well, I don't want your connection with him to get messed up. So, get an alderman or two to deny requests about building up the area."

"Ok."

"If you can convince those who don't like you in public to do it, it will be that more hidden."

"I have an idea. Let me work it from my angle."

"Our goal is to make sure The Africology House is the go-to place. We won't be able to get all the leaders in the city, but we can form a roundtable and systematically put us at the head of the table."

Chanokh asks, "on another note, have you come up with a different name for The Africology House?"

"Not yet." Cue looks as if he just came up with an idea, "I wonder if we can put some sisters on Nathan as well. How strong is he when it comes to them?"

"That's a vicious tactic."

"Vicious, but history has shown that many men have been taken out because of their lust for women." Cue grins and decides, "I will send a few at him. This should distract him even more."

***

Mayor Chanokh sets up a meeting between Cue and the Enlightened Mason's Grand Master Pierre. They meet at The House of Africology's café in Midtown. It is designed as a gathering place, where great minds can meet to discuss business. It has a kitchen and counter display of desserts from different corners of the world. They also make their own desserts and other food items like found in a restaurant.

Chanokh arrives early. He does his normal mayor greetings, speaking to the customers in the café.

Pierre arrives first. They discuss a matter of concern to Pierre while they wait for Cue.

Pierre is a tall slender black man. He's wearing a gray sports jacket, dark Prada blue jeans, a white t-shirt, and red Armani Exchange sneakers.

When Cue arrives, Chanokh quickly rises to greet him at the door.

Pierre looks in a curious manner, wondering why the mayor jumped up so quickly for Cue.

They walk towards Pierre who his standing on the side.

"Mr. Pierre, this is Cue. I consider him to be one of my greatest teachers."

Pierre now realizes why the mayor moved so fast. "Ah you must be a great man, Mr. Cue. Our mayor is doing an excellent job for our city, and if I heard him right, he learned a lot from you."

"I'm pleased to meet you Mr. Pierre."

"Call me brother."

"Okay, Brother Pierre. I've heard a few great things about you as well. Your leadership seems to be remarkable. We could possibly learn a few things from each other."

"Possibly, well, let's find a seat. I'm interested to learn why you wanted to meet me here."

Chanokh, Cue, and Pierre find a booth off in the corner.

Pierre sits down while saying "HuRah."

Cue asks, "what does that mean?"

"It's a saying we had in the Army."

"You were in the Army?"

"Yeah, and that's where I became a traveling man."

"You're talking about the Masons, when you say traveling man, right?

"Yessir."

"I heard so many conspiracies about the Masons, how they control everything like the government."

"Big Brother, how the Mayor jumped up as you arrived, you seem to have taken a page from the Masons, the same conspiracies seem to be doing you well."

Cue looks at him with an upset face. "What are you saying?"

"In short, you got the mayor in your pocket, and I need some of the wealth."

Chanokh responds, "no one has me in their pocket."

"Could have fooled me," Pierre adds. "Let's stop wasting time. What do you want with me?"

"My man," Cue answers.

Pierre slouches slightly in his chair. He squints his eyes.

Cue calmly answers, "I want to know how we can work together to make this city run smoothly."

Pierre answers, "there was a group who once helped develop nearly every country known to man today. This group was responsible for developing what the economists call the Mercantile system where New York Mercantile Exchange got its name from."

Cue interrupts to let Pierre know that he knows about the stock market and its history with black people, "and the first stocks to be traded around the world were black people during slavery."

Pierre nods in agreement, "the group I'm referring to migrated throughout Europe, even being kicked out of Spain with the Moors in 1492 AD. At one point, they were in France. They were prosecuted by the local rulers, mostly because of their wealth of knowledge and currency. They fled for their lives to Scotland, where some of them where already established and well respected. Scotland and Ireland gave homage to them, showing it by giving them leadership positions.

When the queen of England died, she had no heir to take the throne. So, the people sought out the Scottish king to sit on the throne. He was a part of the lineage of the group. He was taught a special doctrine and sanctioned the former queen's son."

Chanokh interrupts, "I thought she didn't have a son."

"In front of the people, she didn't have children, but she had two sons."

"Why wouldn't she acknowledge her two sons?"

"Have you ever heard the royals ask if the baby is too dark to sit on the throne?"

"No."

"Well let me continue."

Chanokh agrees.

"The king sanctioned the son to create a book that would entertain the subjects at the same time coding the generational wealth, in other words, lessons taught since the beginning of time. The key was to code it, where those who were found worthy could see it and learn the lessons taught by those who walked before them."

Cue asks, "for those who weren't found worthy, what would they get, since they had the same access to the information?"

"They would be entertained."

"I see."

"I'll call the group, the initiates. The initiates knew that they would always be prosecuted, since the people of their modern time, especially the leadership, were impatient, unwilling to take the proper steps which always start at the beginning, and working their way up to uncover the answers. Thus, the initiates kept hiding the sacred knowledge.

The Europeans kept unveiling certain information, but the initiates were always 30 steps ahead of them. So, the Europeans created a thing that wouldn't allow the initiates the ability to code their knowledge."

Cue curiously asks, "which was?"

"They created the concept of race, making the initiates look like they were a part of other black people who weren't found worthy."

"All black people aren't worthy?" Chanokh inquires.

"Not at all."

"How do you know them not to be worthy?"

"We have our methods."

Cue responds, "you have caught my interest. I'm not a traveling man, so I don't expect you to give up any pertinent information. But can you share one method?"

"Just because you're not a traveling man, doesn't mean I can't teach you. One of the methods we use is calculating a person's birthdate."

Cue shakes his head in disgust, "numerology."

"Right, which was called arithmetic in ancient times. There are several numerology methods. We use the Rule of 9, the Egyptian, and Chaldean methods."

"I once met a man who used numbers. We didn't get along."

"You didn't get along because your vibrations repelled each other. We all don't get along. It's an energy thing.

In our order, we read the energy that can attract or repel each other, by using the number systems. With that being said, be cautious of who you get in bed with."

"What do you mean?"

"The moral to my story is, I am in the long lineage just like those who kept hiding the info."

"Is that why you are a Mason?"

"Yep, it is my ancestor's system."

"But the Euro-Americans have branches too," implies Cue.

"This is why it's important to study history and correlate actions regardless how much distance is between them. To enter certain colleges in England, one had to take an oath to Christ. These people believed in the power of the oath."

"But Scotland, I'm presuming they didn't have to take an oath," Chanokh asks.

"Bingo, Scottish were more concerned with universal knowledge, not who one worshipped."

"You mentioned Egyptian numerology," Cue disgust for Dr. Freeman now made sense. Their energy didn't align.

"There are many creation stories that have come out of her."

"Her?"

"Egypt."

"Oh"

"One of the stories was about Atum-Re. The sound Atum-Re made when humans were created was Hu spelled HW."

"Oh Hu-man, is that where they got it."

"Could be, that would be for you to research. I only share the methods and introductory information. It's up to those who may be worthy to uncover the rest."

Everyone sits silent for a moment.

"Well Mr. Pierre, I appreciate the info you shared and would still like to find out how we can work together."

"Do you mean the mayor, as well, because we already have approached him on some issues in our community. We haven't received a response yet?"

"Bureaucracy, I can't give too much special attention to one group over others."

"He's right, I learned this during the process of opening Club Nefer."

"Interesting, well my brother, I will say again, be cautious of who you get in bed with." Pierre knows that Cue and Chanokh have connected with the people who run the city. "Fellas, the type of knowledge within the craft is like krypto to superman."

"You mean Kryptonite."

"That's it. The sacred knowledge of Africa."

***

Pierre returns from the restroom. "Well, I'm going to get up out of here. It was a pleasure meeting the two of you here."

Cue responds, "the pleasure was mine."

Chanokh nods in agreement.

Pierre shakes their hands and begins walking out of the door. Several people stand up and follow him out.

Cue rocks his head back. "I guess, he was prepared for any trouble."

"I guess so," expresses Chanokh.

When Pierre and his entourage get outside, he says, "they are deep in bed with the elites of this city. We're gonna have to keep our eyes on them. We don't need any surprises."

"How was the vibration?" One of the men asks.

"They struck a bad chord, but there's a possibility that they can be flipped."

"People like them are always dangerous," another man recognizes.

"Without a doubt, especially those who think their enemy is their friend."

CHAPTER 6

Nathan is sitting at his desk when his cellphone rings, "yes, may I help you?"

"Elder, how are you doing today?"

"Ah, Stephen, I'm well, and how are you doing?"

"I'm well too."

"So, what do I give the honor of this phone call to?"

"I know it seems like I only call when I want something."

Nathan quickly interrupts before Stephen makes any more excuses. He doesn't have much time to give to Stephen. "There's no need to add the introduction. What's going on?"

"Well elder, a few of my business partners and I attempted to put a lounge in zip code 53206."

"Okay."

"It was denied by the common council."

"Did you talk directly to Alderman Davis?"

"No."

"Let me explain why it's important to talk directly to the alderperson of the district you are attempting to put a business in. There are times that the alderperson feels like they are god. They want respect. Sometimes it's difficult to know which one has the god-complex. So, it's good to cover all angles, and approach the alderperson before making any serious moves."

"But we went through the proper paperwork."

"I get it, but these people are the ones who say if they want it in their district or not. They will find all the excuses or find all the reasons why something should happen. You always speak directly to them first."

"I see where we messed up. Well thanks for your insight elder."

"My pleasure." Nathan hangs up the phone right in time to receive a call from Robert. "Robert, how's Egypt?"

"As Mischel says, 'it's like being in paradise. We've been in upper Egypt, mostly Luxor so far. The temples are amazing, but I must admit the face manipulation of the statues and sculptors is quite disturbing."

"I understand."

"Elder, a thought came to mind, while we were flying close to the pyramids."

"What's that?"

"Instead of doing shipping container style houses, we should think about pyramid and yurt structures. The energy coming from the circle and the triangular shape will be next level."

"The double helix just came to mind," responds Nathan.

"I sent you an email of the 3-story white pyramid house, and a yurt divided into a living room, 3 bedrooms, 2 bathrooms, and a kitchen."

Mischel walks into the room, "who are you talking to?"

"Elder Nathan."

"Tell him I said hello, even though it took several days for us to be able to contact him."

Robert chuckles, "my wife says hello even though it took several days."

"It's okay, I know you are on your honeymoon."

"He says it's okay, he knows that we are on our honeymoon."

Mischel smirks at Robert.

Nathan hears Mischel say in the background, "I still can't believe you Robert. All I asked you to do was make sure our phones had the international call plan set up."

Nathan laughs, "oh oh, you done went and messed up already."

"Yeah, I know, and I'm not going to hear the end of it for a while." Robert looks at Mischel and asks, "what are you up too."

"Playing with the word Luxor. Put Nathan on the speaker phone, I have a question for him."

Robert puts him on speaker phone.

"Nathan, I'm using the Rule of Nine to play with the name Luxor."

Nathan replies, "and what have you come up with?"

"Well, I didn't lower the numbers to its natural number."

"OK."

"L is 12, U is 21, X is 24, O is 15, and R is 18. I added 12 and 21 which is 33. I left the X alone. Then I added 15 and 18, which is 33. The pattern here is 33-24-33."

"That's interesting because it reminds me of two books written by Schwaller de Lubicz called *The Temple of Man* and *The Temple in Man.*"

"Tell me more."

"Let me read the description of the book. According to part of *The Temple of Man's* description," Nathan begins reading, "Schwaller de Lubicz's *stone-by-stone survey of the temple of Amun-Mut-Khonsu at Luxor allows us to step into the mentality of Ancient Egypt and experience the Egyptian way of thinking within the context of their own worldview.*

His study finds the temple to be an eloquent expression and summary--an architectural encyclopedia--of what the Egyptians knew of humanity and the universe. Through a reading of the temple's measures and proportions, its axes and orientations, and the symbolism and placement of its bas-reliefs, along with the accompanying studies of related medical and mathematical papyri, Schwaller de Lubicz demonstrates how advanced the civilization of Ancient Egypt was, a civilization that possessed exalted knowledge and achievements both materially and spiritually. In so doing, Schwaller de Lubicz effectively demonstrates that Ancient Egypt, not Greece, is at the base of Western science, civilization, and culture.

To understand the temple of Luxor, twelve years of field work were undertaken with the utmost exactitude by Schwaller de Lubicz in collaboration with French archaeologist Clement Robichon and the respected Egyptologist Alexandre Varille. From this work were produced over 1000 pages of text and proofs of the sacred geometry of the temple and 400 illustrations and photographs that make up The Temple of Man.

The Temple of Man is a monument to inspired insight, conscientious scholarship, and exacting archaeological groundwork that represents a major contribution to humanity's perennial search for self-knowledge and the prehistoric origins of its culture and science."

"What do the numbers mean?" Mischel asks.

Nathan responds, "the numbers can mean many things. The 33 can be pillars of a master teacher giving a master lesson. The 24 can be a lesson of a strong partnership foundation based on the 4 being persistence, stability, or organization and the two being partnership." Nathan pauses and continues, "when reduced to its natural number we see 6-6-6. Although many Christians view this number as the mark of the beast, some numerologists explain this number as the perfect man or human which makes sense why the study of the Temple of *Amun-Mut-Khonsu* would be called *The Temple of and in Man*."

Mischel excitingly responds, "I must learn more about these numbers. But first I must get my husband to understand the importance of his part in our partnership."

Nathan laughs.

"You know I still love you," Robert strategically maneuvers his affection for her.

"I love you too, but that isn't going to get you out of this hot water."

Robert says, "Nathan let me call you another time. I may not live this one down."

Nathan understandably says, "welcome to the married life, my brother."

***

Awhile later, Robert hears Mischel in the kitchen. They are staying in an AirBNB. The price they received for their stay in Egypt is incredibly inexpensive, since Mischel chose to go the nontraditional route.

Robert walks into the kitchen, "are you still mad?"

"I was never mad. I was annoyed."

"I'll do better next time."

"I trust you will," confidently responds Mischel.

Curiously Robert asks, "what are you making?"

"I'm making us a new smoothie. I call it Lover to represent us."

"A new smoothie, how exciting."

Mischel laughs as she continues to put the ingredients in. "Why don't you go relax in the other room? I'll be done soon."

"Okay." Robert goes to sit on the balcony. He wants to ask her about her new usage of numerology.

Mischel walks on the balcony, handing Robert the smoothie. She stands over him while he takes a sip.

"This is good, baby."

Mischel smiles and sits next to him. They cuddle, looking out in the distance at the spectacular sites in Egypt.

"So let me ask you..."

"Okay."

"It seems like you've been playing with the numbers a lot."

"I have."

"What else have you come up with?"

Mischel cuddles to Robert tighter. "Matter of fact, I wanted to talk to you about this."

Robert smiles.

"Instead of calling the readings, the life path for the birth date, the soul for the vowels, the outer personality for the consonants, and the destiny for the complete name, I was thinking about calling the birth date the destiny because it is the only fixed number.

I realized that when I added your last name to mine. I imagined how many people are out of alignment with who they are because they change their name."

"I'm not quite understanding."

"Think about this, before Dr. Freeman introduced us to numerology, I was a wreck. I didn't understand the energy that was flowing through me. It caused me to allow other unhealthy energy streams to flow through me. If I knew my purpose and who I was from the start, I would have been more focused on that, eliminating unwanted energies."

Robert moves to look into Mischel's eyes. He's intrigued of what she's saying. "So, people are basically being pushed and pulled in directions because they don't understand the importance of the vibration of their birth name."

"Even worse, what if their parents argued about the name at birth. The wrong soul could have entered the body."

"That's a horrible thought, although I don't doubt it couldn't happen."

They sit silent for a while.

Then Mischel continues to explain her latest thought. "I would keep the soul's name the same. I think the soul is a bunch of gathered energy, and energy is the spirit."

"I get it."

"I would change the outer personality to just personality because it's the character of the person seen by others. And I would change the destiny to expression because it is all the numbers of the name together."

"I was thinking about changing the life path number to the life task number, but I like your idea of destiny instead. It gives more of a focal point. Also, I would change the expression to true potential. If someone changed their name, I would call it the present potential."

Mischel smiles. "So. we should use Destiny number, Soul number, Personality number and True potential or present potential instead of Life Path, Soul, Outer Personality, and Destiny."

"I agree. Let me ask, how would you explain all the numbers assisting you to the destiny."

"For now, since change seems to be constant, I would explain the soul as the best energy used to get to the destiny. The others I have to give more thought to."

Robert kisses Mischel's forehead. "Well, I love your idea. I think we should work on incorporating it into our new projects. We will keep everything open, in BETA, as we continue to uncover the lessons of the universe."

***

Several hours later Mischel and Robert venture out into the street.

"Look at that bird," Mischel points towards the east.

"That's strange," replies Robert.

The bird is long, white with black in its wings, and has dark plumes on the lower back and a bare black head and neck.

They continue to walk. As a short darkskin man approaches them. He is accompanied by a small baboon. He heads in their direction but stops before he gets to them. He shows them a book which looks to be a Islamic Qur'an.

Mischel comments, "we should get one as a souvenir."

"Okay, I'll ask him for one." Robert looking at the baboon, walks over to the man and waves. He places his left hand on his chest and bows his head.

The man looks and smiles, giving him a Qur'an.

Robert replies, ""shukran lak (thank you in Arabic)."

The man smiles again and says in English, "you are welcome." Then swiftly walks away.

Robert shrugs his shoulders not knowing why the man quickly left. He walks back to Mischel without looking at the book. He hands it to her.

"Numerology, I thought it was a Qur'an."

"Wait, what? Let me see that baby," responds Robert.

Mischel hands him the book.

He begins to examine it. Then he begins to think of the instruction that Dr. Freeman gave him about looking for the man with the red collar. Robert doesn't remember if he had a red collar on or not.

"Are you alright?" Mischel asks.

"I'm fine. Do you remember if he had a red collar?"

"I wasn't paying attention."

"I hope he wasn't the one I was supposed to meet." Robert starts flipping through the book. He stops at a picture, reading the name aloud, "Muhammad ibn Musa al-Khawarizmi." He then reads the name under the second picture, "Ya'qub ibn Ishaq al-Sabah al-Kindi."

Mischel asks, "does it say who they are?"

Robert flips to the next page and reads, "Al-Khawarizmi and al-Kindi are responsible for introducing the symbols which we call numbers to the Europeans."

"Wow that's interesting."

Robert skims the page. He tilts his head like something is strange. "It says al-Khawarizmi wrote Jewish calendars. That's strange that an Arab would author a Jewish calender."

"Yeah, that's very strange."

"Now, I'm curious to what's really going on."

In agreeance Mischel says, "me too."

CHAPTER 7

Mischel and Robert arrive at the Coptic Church, which is a museum.

After being curious of what the word Coptic means, Mischel begins reading the Coptic Museum website on her cellphone. "The term 'Copt' refers to the Egyptian Christian who were evangelized by Sr. Mark the Apostle in the first century A.D. The word probably originates from the old Egyptian word Hwt-Ka-Ptah which means the "House of the God, Ptah." While the Greeks used the word Aigyptos for Egypt, the Copts used the Copitc term Kyptos.

"That's interesting," responds Robert.

As Robert looks over Mischel's shoulder, she continues scrolling through the website, they are distracted by several men not of African descent walking out of the Museum carrying something.

Robert whispers to Mischel, "is that an artifact?"

"I don't know."

Then a man standing close to them responds, "it is what you think it is."

Robert turns towards him. He is the man who gave them the numerology book. "Ah, it's you again."

"It is I," the man laughs as if he is quoting a movie line.

Robert recognizes that the man is wearing a red collar. "A red collar," slips out of his mouth.

"This old thing? Some man from the United States gave this to me several decades ago, saying when it's time someone will recognize it." The man pauses and looks closely at Robert and Mischel. "You are the only one who has ever recognized it."

Robert gives the first sign of the Huda, but the man doesn't respond. "What's your name good sir?"

"I'm Idham Ibn Khalid and you?"

"I'm Robert, and she is my wife Mischel."

"I'm glad to meet the two of you."

"The pleasure is ours," replies Robert.

"There's no need for you to go into the museum. I have something that may be much more interesting."

Robert looks at Mischel. She nods as if to say let's check it out.

"Come with me. The man who gave me this collar also told me I was to show the person who asked a sacred place in Egypt known only by the guardians," explains Idham.

Robert knew at this point that the man received the information from the Brotherhood of Huda. Robert was beginning to ask the man, if he was a part. When all of a sudden, gunshots rang out.

Robert, Mischel, and Idham fall to the ground.

"That's them," a voice rings out, as a group of people in white jalabiya and Keffiyeh began running towards them holding what looks to be AK-15s.

"Come, come," Idham calmly suggests.

The group gets closer, as Mischel, Robert, and Idham scuffled to their feet. Idham led the way to a side door of the Coptic Museum. "Come. Do you have your ankh?"

Robert looks a Mischel as if he is hesitant.

Mischel looks back at Robert as if they have no choice.

Robert nods. He follows Idham through the door. Mischel is closely behind.

The door closes without a sound. There is another door, over it the words read "***Let No One Ignorant of Numerology Enter Here!!!***"

Robert pulls out his ankh with the djed pillar in the center.

"Place it here. If it works, we are saved. If not, we are doomed" explains Idham.

Robert slides his ankh in the wall. A door opens, allowing all three of them to walk through. When they are inside, the door closes behind them without a sound.

***

Nathan walks down the streets of downtown Milwaukee. He is enjoying the architecture of the buildings, some built as early as the beginning of the 1900s. He thinks to himself, "with all the poverty spoken of, one wouldn't even consider that Milwaukee is actually a beautiful city." He continues to stroll when someone taps him on his shoulder.

"Elder Nathan,"

Startled Nathan turns, "yes."

"My name is Pierre. I'm the Grand Master of the Enlighten Masons. You may have heard of us."

"I've heard many good things about your work."

"I've also heard many good things about the research of the Africology House."

"Well son, I'm no longer apart of the Africology House. My work is being conducted in The House of Africology now."

Pierre nods his head, as if, accepting the correction by Nathan. "The reason I stopped you elder, is to inform you that you have a snag in your plans for your project."

"Project."

"Yes, my inside man has told me that the mayor is trying to get support to stop your 30th Street Corridor project. And if I were a betting man, I would bet that Cue has something to do with it."

"I met Cue several years ago." Nathan hesitates but knows that Pierre is well aware of the lodge systems, since he is a Freemason. So, he continues his train of thought, "I've just learned that my old colleague gave him his position of the Sovereign Grand Priest over The Africology House."

"Jacob Moletree."

"Yes."

"That's interesting."

Nathan looks at Pierre and smiles. "I do appreciate the information."

"You know elder, I have inside people, but I don't have that number 5 person yet."

"Number 5, I'm assuming you mean a fixer."

"Exactly, I need a person who is a game changer." Pierre looks deep into Nathan's eyes and continues, "you know that person who has a go with the flow mentality, with the ability to understand everyone who he or she comes in contact with, while working to get our agenda accepted."

Nathan smiles again, "you definitely need that type of person on your team, especially in your position of a Grand Master. You can't get your hands dirty. I hope you trust your insider or at least have a go between person, so the insider doesn't have direct communication with you?"

"My insider definitely passed the information through a third party."

"Good, because the moves I make, I don't want you to get caught in the middle. Your work is crucial."

Pierre curiously inquires, "my work."

"Yes, your work, the youth are still interested in receiving information that the craft has in their possession."

"Are you a traveling man?"

"No, not in the way that you are. But I have been through initiations and rituals receiving similar information."

"Really?" Pierre asks.

"No one has a monopoly on ancient information. We all simply choose to share the information with those who we find worthy. Like the KKK, it only took one member to be a part of the craft and share the information with the other Knights. This in no way means the KKK where a part of your great order."

"Agreed, they simply shared the information of universal principles."

Nathan is impressed with Pierre's understanding. "You should come by The House of Africology sometime. I would like to introduce you to Mischel and Robert. If you're married bring your wife. Family is the key to advance our people."

"I agree and would like that."

Nathan hands Pierre a business card, "Mischel and Robert should be back in town in about 2 weeks. Call me then, so we can make some type of dinner arrangement."

Pierre writes down his number, "I don't carry a business card, but here's my number, so you know it's me calling." Pierre puts out his hand to shake Nathan's hand.

Nathan shakes Pierre's hand. They nod and walk in separate directions.

***

Mischel closed all her businesses, before she married Robert. She hired her cousin, Mahogani, to run the Midtown building now called the Tama-Re Empowerment Center.

A yurt shape was added to the Tama-Re Empowerment Center. An Egyptian Ankh was placed on top of the Yurt. Below the Ankh, there were paintings of different symbols found on the Dendera Zodiac Calendar. The House of Africology wanted everyone to know that the

Empowerment Center revolved around an African theme.

The House of Africology was also working on getting a charter school, but the Department of Education did not approve it, yet. This didn't stop the center. In the meantime, they had a tutoring program to allow young people to receive an entire year of schooling.

For the young people to be a part, their parents had to go through the process with the state of Wisconsin, showing their children were being homeschooled. The tutoring program was operating on a $1.2 million budget. This wasn't a lot for the program. However, this is all Nathan, Robert, and Mischel were able to solicit through fundraising, at the time.

Mahogani accepted a new class of students. This was the center's largest participation yet. Twenty-five students enrolled.

The House of Africology members decided not to allow any class to have more than 33 students.

Since Mahogani directed the center, she introduced herself and what to expect from the program. As she finishes her presentation, she asks "does anyone have any questions?"

"Ms. Mahogani, I have a question." The young girl raises her hand and blurts out at the same time.

"Ok, but next time raise your hand, before you say anything. Allow your tutor to recognize you. What's your name?"

"Yes, ma'am. My name is Aliyah." Aliyah is wearing a dress. Her hair has long curls.

"Please ask your question."

"With what this program offers, will we be ready for college?"

"Oh yeah, you will be beyond prepared for college." Mahogani says. She lowers her voice, "rumor has it some people are working on building a college and creating some businesses. In case, all of you want to stay and be a part of our program." Mahogani looks around the room, some of the children's eyes get big. A couple of the children seem skeptical.

Another hand raises.

"Yes, sir," Mahogani acknowledges him.

"That can't happen. Black people will never get anything in this country."

"Where did you hear that," Mahogani asks.

"My uncle and his friends talk about how America mistreats black people all the time." The little boy is wearing a polo shirt, tucked in his pants. His hair is neatly cut with a part on the side.

"What's your name, young brother?"

"My name is Hakeem."

"Well Brother Hakeem, if that were true you wouldn't be sitting here now. Have you looked at all the accomplishments The House of Africology has completed in this city?"

"No, ma'am. I never heard of it until my mother signed me up for this program a couple of days ago."

Mahogani slightly nods her head. "Well, Hakeem keep your eyes open. You will see and experience some amazing things."

Hakeem a little disappointed says, "yes, ma'am."

"Are there any more questions?"

Hakeem leans over and whispers to the boy next to him, "this isn't real."

The boy shrugs his shoulders not saying a word.

"Well, if there's no more questions, enjoy the rest of your day." Mahogani gathers her things. As she walks out, she says to the tutor, "thank you for allowing me to speak to your group. If you need anything, just let me know."

"Yes, ma'am."

Mahogani walks down the hall. She shines bright, smiling from ear to ear as she acknowledges the décor of the hallway.

***

"Alright class, let's get back to our first lesson."

"Brother Hill, I agree with Hakeem. Black people can't do nothing in this country," Eddie is slightly taller than the others. He wears his hair in lots. They look as if he just started growing them.

"Well Eddie, some black people can't. Other black people do a lot. The black people that do a lot aren't usually spoken of." Chris Hill is in his mid-thirties. He is about 5 feet 8 inches tall. He is an Army Veteran. He wears the center's uniform, which is a black shirt with the Tama-Re logo and khakis.

The first-year students aren't allowed to wear the uniform. When they reach their second year, they will be required to wear it. The key for the uniform is to demonstrate their accomplishment of gaining knowledge and showing pride, as they represent the center. Also, the first-year students aren't allowed to wear the uniform, because they don't know how to properly explain the vision and mission of the center, as of yet.

"My goal is to teach you how to be successful in this world. Black people aren't the only ones who struggle. This is the first thing you must get out of your mind," Bro. Hill exclaims, "America wasn't designed to take care of people."

"So, what was it designed for Brother Hill," Tiara asks. Tiara is short. She's wearing a matching short set and brand-new tennis shoes. Her hair is braided to her shoulders.

"I'm glad you asked Tiara. It was designed to be a platform for people to physically experiment with new ideas. It allows the opportunity to build something."

"Everyone but the slaves," expresses Hakeem.

"Hakeem, you do know not all black people during that time were slaves."

Hakeem looks disgusted.

"That's not what we were taught in school," yells out another girl with short hair, wearing glasses.

"I wasn't taught about the other black people either, Diamond."

Diamond wears glasses and her hair in a short afro.

Brother Hill continues, "I was introduced to the idea that not all black people were slaves several years ago, and I began doing my own research. Researching information after it is given to you becomes your responsibility. In this day and age, it's easy to research information because of the internet."

"But Brother Hill, who were some of the blacks who weren't slaves?" Diamond asks.

"That was one of the lessons I had planned to teach in the future. But there was a group called the Freemen."

A sigh is heard from different students around the classroom.

"After doing some research about these free black people, I asked myself why they didn't have to show documentation of not being a slave like black people released from slavery. I haven't uncovered the answer yet, but with further research, I know I will find the answer."

Jasmine says, "I'm excited to learn more from you Brother Hill." Jasmine wears her hair in an afro-style. She has a braid hanging from both sides.

"Jasmine, it will be my pleasure to teach each of you. Let's get back to the lesson."

The students seem much more intense, after the brief interaction.

***

"Hi, my name is Derrick." Derrick introduces himself to another student from his class, sitting on a bench dribbling a basketball.

George doesn't say a word.

"My fault, I just wanted to introduce myself."

"It's cool. I'm just in deep concentration, checkin out the people in our class."

"Oh, so what did you think about Brother Hill's lesson on energy?"

"My father taught me that years ago. But it shows Brother Hill knows his stuff. He's sharing the beginning of things. I hope he goes into the power of the mind."

Derrick, shocked, says, "the power of the mind. What does the mind have to do with anything?"

"My father tells me over and over again that 'when man permits his thoughts and desires to be formed in the likeness of impressions received from without, he will be more or less controlled by the environment, and he will be in the hands of fate, but when he changes every impression he encounters from without into an original idea and incorporates that idea into a new mental image, he uses the environment as a servant, thereby placing fate in his own hands.'"

"What does that mean?

"I don't have a clue, but I hope Brother Hill can explain it to me."

They both laugh.

CHAPTER 8

Idham, Mischel, and Robert go through some kind of energy field. Mischel and Robert look at Idham, as his appearance transforms.

They eventually arrive at an unknown location.

"Where are we," Robert asks.

"We are in the land of Aramat."

Robert curiously questions, "Aramat, what is it?"

"We are in the underworld. The land underneath the land which you call earth. Your people would consider this a subterranean city."

Mischel staring at Idham asks, "my question is how did you change, Idham? You look much different."

"I am home. This is my real appearance." Idham head has transformed into the shape of a cone. His eyes look like he is Asian, but he has the same golden-brown complexion, as he did in Egypt. "You will see different beings down here. So don't be too alarmed."

"Different beings?"

"Yes, you will see the Teros and the Deros. I belong to the Teros clan. Our head shape looks like mine. The Deros have an elephant trunk for a nose. Many of the adults are obese."

As Idham was speaking a little creature walks by. It looks like a porcupine, because its hair stands straight up all over its body.

Mischel shrieks, "what's that?"

The creature looks a Mischel. It shakes its head in disgust. "I'm a Duwaani."

"I am so sorry. I just..."

"It's okay. You are obviously an earthling who lacks knowledge. I've studied your people for many centuries. You have a lot to learn." The Duwaani walks away.

Mischel feels horrible. Robert rubs her arm assuring her that everything is alright.

Idham says, "let me take you to the center of our land. This is where the original book called *The Distinguished Teachings of Thoth* rests."

Robert excitingly replies, "I once had that book in my possession."

"A man by the name of Ahkhah recently brought the scroll back to the library. He said new information had been added. It has been a hot attraction as it sits in a glass case."

Robert looks at Mischel. They don't say a word.

Mischel asks, "can we go see it?"

They walk through the streets. Above them is a sun. Mischel and Robert wonder how a sun was in the middle of the earth.

Idham notices them looking at the sun. "Don't gaze to long at the sun. It will blind you."

They walk through the streets. They see all types of different beings. It's like a trading center where people of different cultures living on earth meet to conduct business.

"That's it up ahead," Idham says.

The building is 3 glass domes. In the center of the middle dome is a purple light beaming upwards.

Robert nods at Mischel as to say that's it.

***

Nathan goes to city hall. He received the letter denying the property in the 30th Street Corridor section of town. He may have been upset, if Pierre didn't give him a heads up.

Nathan had time to strategize his next move. As he walks towards City Hall, he sees the mayor, but the mayor doesn't notice him. "Good morning, Mr. Mayor."

Startled Chanokh looks at him like a deer in headlights.

Nathan continues, "there's no need to worry. This is all business. Nothing is personal."

"I'm glad you recognize that everything is about business," replies Chanokh.

"I do. I was just curious to what will be put in the place that you once promised us?"

"Someone out bid you for the spot. They are putting up a manufacturing company that will hire locals."

"Oh, that's good."

"I thought so myself."

"Well, I think we can cancel our meeting, since we talked face-to-face as men."

"Are you sure?"

"I'm quite sure. But I do want to leave you with these words I memorized several decades ago:

'When you see evil do not form ideas that are in the likeness of that evil; do not think of the evil as bad, but try to understand the forces that are back of that evil-- forces that are good in themselves, though misdirected in their present state. By trying to understand the nature of the power that is back of evil or adversity, you will not form bad ideas, and therefore will feel no bad effects from experiences that may seem undesirable. At the same time, you will think your own thought about the experiences, thereby developing the power of the MASTER MIND.'"

"What are you trying to say, sir? Are you saying someone is controlling my mind?"

Nathan smirks, "I'm not saying anything. I was just repeating it to myself as I was walking to your building and decided to share it with you." Nathan knew the statement would rattle Chanokh. Very few men want to be known as a man who another man is controlling.

***

Robert, Mischel, and Idham arrive at the library. There are at least 20 different beings staring into the library.

They hear someone question, "is that the scroll of all scrolls?"

Another voice says, "yes, it was taken from the library many sun cycles ago, to assist the land dwellers above. But, they mishandled it."

"What do you mean mishandled it? Who could mishandle something so precious?"

"The who are the land dwellers. They lack the master minds of old. The old master minds shared the information with those who we here would call less worthy. When they shared it, the unworthy took the information and made it their own."

Robert looks at Mischel in a curious way.

"Did the master minds share everything in the scroll?"

"No, but rumor has it that they shared just enough to allow the unworthy to have the upper hand over other land dwellers."

Robert asks, "what did they give them?"

"The science of the number 7."

Robert leans over to Mischel and whispers in her ear, "we must study the science of the number 7."

Mischel nods in agreement.

Idham, Mischel, and Robert walk away from the crowd.

"Idham what do you know about the science of the number 7," inquires Robert.

"The land dwellers claim it is the science taught by Hermes."

"Hermes is the Greek, Jewish, and other people's replacement for the Supreme Grand Master Tehuti," express Mischel.

Idham responds, "you are right."

"But Tehuti taught the science of the number 9," adds Robert.

Idham affirms, "yes."

"That means the science of the number 7 isn't as powerful as the science of the number 9," states Mischel.

"But it's powerful enough to rule the world," Robert agrees with her. "Idham, does the library allow beings to read the scroll."

"Only those who are a part of the Priesthood of Huda. Yet, Huda is so secretive that we don't know if any are here or not. I can only assume

Ahkhah was a member of Huda, but he is long gone."

"I see."

"Sorry to disappoint you. A rumor is floating around that all the members of Huda were assassinated by the Aaronites. These are the ones who now use the science of the number 7 to rule above."

Robert makes it seem like he is disappointed. He knows for sure that Idham has no clue that Mischel and him are a part of Huda.

"Let's go to our dwelling for the night. I will introduce you to one of the leaders of our great land Aramat tomorrow. .

CHAPTER 9

"Since we are using modern numerology or the Rule of 9, I would like 9 students to come to the board and breakdown your first name," Brother Hill gives the instructions for the next activity. "Are there any volunteers?"

Jasmine raises her hand.

"SiStar Jasmine, come to the board and show us how to do this."

Jasmine walks to the chalkboard. She writes her first name. She separates the vowels from the consonants.

1   9   5

J A S M I N E

1   1 4   5

"Great job! You can continue to add your vowels and consonants."

Jasmine writes:

1+9+5= 15

1+5= 6

1+1+4+5= 11

1+1= 2

15+11= 26

2+6= 8

Brother Hill says, "you did the entire equation. I first only wanted you to write the vowel and consonant numbers. Then explain each in your own words."

"I'm sorry Brother Hill. Can I still explain them?"

"By all means."

"Well, my vowels equal 15. When I reduce the number by adding the 1 & 5, I get the number 6. The number 6 means I lookout for my family and my community."

"Excellent."

Jasmine continues, "the consonants in my name equal the number 11. I did the same with my consonants as I did my vowels. I added the 1 and 1 which equal the number 2."

Brother Hill interrupts, "before you continue, you must know that the number 11 is a master number. This usually means that you don't reduce the number. The numbers 22, 33, 44, 55, 66, 77, 88, and 99 are also master numbers. But continue with explaining the number 2."

"Yessir, the number 2 in the position of the consonants means people see me as a partner. They may think of me as a leader behind the scenes."

"Excellent, I'll explain the master number 11 as a person who is a master at inspiring others. So, if it is seen in the consonant's position, people are inspired by you. They may come to you for an inspiring or motivating word." Brother Hill turns towards the class, "not everyone has a master number in their name. In like manner, no one always vibrates in a master number frequency. Jasmine is right because when she isn't vibrating on a master level. She will be vibrating as a person who cooperates with others. You can continue to explain your work, Jasmine."

"I did my own research. I learned that the next step is to add the number 15 to the number 11. They equal 26. Next, I add the 2 and 6 which is 8. The number 8 has several meanings. One meaning is infinity. I also found that it is a number that attracts energy quickly."

"Karma"

"Yes, that's the word, karma. But Brother Hill, what is karma?"

"Excellent question, I'll explain it this way. When you do something, something else will occur. All of you may have heard terms like reap what you sow, what goes around comes around, cause and effect. The list goes on."

"The number 8 also shows that I could be good at business. This fits perfect with me because one day I want to own my own business."

"According to this number, you have a great potential of doing just that," Brother Hill affirms. "Great job, Jasmine. Who is next?"

No one raises their hand.

"I will pick the next person if no one volunteers. All I want you to do is add the vowels and consonants in your first name. Then explain the numbers. Some of you may have the same numbers as Jasmine, so just repeat what she said."

Eddie raises his hand.

"Good Eddie, please come to the board."

"I'm not too good at this."

"Don't worry, neither was I when I first began. That's why we practice. In the process of practicing, you become the best."

Eddie erases Jasmine's work. Then he writes his name. Then, he writes the numerical value to each letter.

5   9 5

E d d i e

   4 4

Eddie starts to explain, "first I look at my vowels, writing their number value on top and add them. 5+9+5= 19. Then I add the 1 and 9 which is 10 and the 1 and 0 which is 1. My vowel number is one.

The consonants are next. I put the number value under my name. 4+4= 8." Eddie starts walking to his desk.

Brother Hill says, "Um, Brother Eddie."

"Yessir."

"You forgot to explain what each number means."

"Oh yeah, I forgot. The number one means I can be a leader. I focus on the individual self. And the number 8 is what Jasmine said but it is in a different place. People see me as a businessperson, where Jasmine's has the potential of being a businessperson."

"Excellent job, Brother Eddie. You can take your seat."

Eddie walks to his desk.

Brother Hill looks at his class roster. He raises his head and says, "for the sake of time, I want Hakeem, Jamal, George, and Derrick to come to the front board and calculate their names."

All four of them walk to the front.

Brother Hill calls, "and Aliyah, Tiara, and Diamond, to calculate their names on the board in the back."

They walk to the back and begin writing their names.

"I will call each one of you, one-by-one, to explain your names."

The young brothers complete the assignment.

---

    1   5 5   (1+5+5= 11)

H A K E E M

7   2   4   (7+2+4= 13; 1+3= 4)

---

1   1   (1+1= 2)

J A M A L

1   4   3   (1+4+3= 8)

---

5   9   (5+9= 14; 1+4= 5)

D E R R I C K

4   99 32 (4+9+9+3+2= 27; 2+7= 9)

---

5 6   5 (5+6+5= 16; 1+6= 7)

G E O R G E

7   9 7   (7+9+7= 23; 2+3= 5)

The siStars also complete the written part of their names.

1 9 1   (1+9+1= 11)

A L I Y A H

3   7 8   (3+7+8= 18; 1+8= 9)

---

9 1 1   (9+1+1= 11)

T I A R A

2   9   (9+2= 11)

---

9 1   6   (9+1+6= 16; 1+6= 7)

D I A M O N D

4   4   5 4   (4+4+5+4= 17; 1+7= 8)

"Great job everyone," congratulates Brother Hill. Let's begin with siStar Diamond."

"Well, my 7-letter name has vowels equaling 7, and my consonants equal 8."

"Let me stop you there siStar Diamond," interrupts Brother Hill. "There's even a process that is used based on the number of letters in your name. You can continue."

Diamond continues, "the number 7 represents the mysteries. A person with this number must go deep beneath the surface of things. And the number 8 is like Brother Eddie said, I am seen as a businessperson."

"Give me a second," Brother Hill requests from the class. He begins writing something. As the class patiently waits. He says, "ok, since some of you have some of the same numbers. I'm going to ask each one of you who didn't go yet to explain the number from your chart which I ask."

Hakeem, Aliyah, Derrick, George, Tiara, and Jamal look at each other.

"Brother Hakeem, explain the number 4 in your chart."

"Well, the number 4 speaks for my character or how others see me. It means I show people that I am organized and persistent."

"Thank you, Brother Hakeem. Let's go with siStar Tiara. Please explain the number 11."

"Which one Brother Hill, I have two."

"You're right, please explain your soul number 11."

"My soul number 11 can mean several things. For example, I came to this world to experience a higher spiritual journey, or I'm motivated by inspiring things."

"Thank you, siStar Tiara. Brother Derrick, please explain the number 5 in your chart."

"I hope I'm right. This is all new to me."

"Brother Derrick, we all experience new things the first time we do them. Take your time and do your best."

"Yessir. The number 5 is my soul number. It means I can relate to every soul number. My soul craves freedom, adventure, and power."

"Excellent job, Brother Derrick," Brother Hill reassures him through his body language. "Who do we have left?"

Aliyah says, "Jamal and me."

George doesn't say anything, since his name wasn't mentioned.

"Who wants to go first?"

"Ladies first, Aliyah can go," replies Jamal.

"SiStar Aliyah, Brother Jamal has given you the floor."

Aliyah looks at Jamal and smiles. "Which one should I do Brother Hill?"

"Your number 9."

"The number 9 is my character number. It's how people see me. They see me as a person who sees the bigger picture of things. The number 9 represents completion." Aliyah hesitates, "I don't know, as of yet, how this explains me."

"We will have many more classes for you to figure that out, siStar Aliyah. Jamal, tell us about your number 2."

"The number 2 represents partnership or companionship. It is the leader behind the scenes. Since, my soul is a number 2, it could mean that I make an excellent partner," Jamal looks at Aliyah and continues, "I have leadership qualities but choose not to be in the front."

"Ok, everyone did an excellent job. You can all go back to your seats."

Jasmine interrupts, "Brother Hill, you forgot about George."

"My apologies Brother George."

"It's ok."

Brother Hill scans his sheet of paper and states, "Brother George, please tell us about your number 5."

"The number 5 is found in my character. I am seen as the person who understands everyone. I can also pull everyone to work together. The number 5 sits in the middle and touches every number."

"Well said Brother George. Did I miss anyone?"

Everyone shakes their heads no.

"Ok, now you can take your seats." Brother Hill waits for everyone to sit down, then explains, "Your first name represents what you have come to teach. The real soul and character numbers are found when you add up the first, middle, and last name that you were given at birth.

There can be an issue with this, if your name was changed soon after birth."

Aliyah quickly raises her hand.

"Yes, siStar Aliyah."

"Why is this?"

"Why is what?"

"Why can there be a serious issue if your name is changed soon after birth?

"Good question, I'll answer it like this. Because your soul found the perfect body to align with, the body is vibrating on a specific frequency. As you are learning each letter has a vibration, and the letters combined put each letter numerical value together to make the best vibration like the perfect music composition.

If the name is changed, the frequency changes leaving the soul aligned with something unfamiliar to itself at the time."

"What can happen?" Aliyah asks further.

"All types of hidden or unhidden mental issues can occur." Brother Hill knows that he has went too far with his explanation, "let me stop here. It's time for your next class."

The students get up to leave the class.

As they walk out Jasmine says to Diamond, "Brother Hill knows a lot. We can learn a lot about what the House of Africology is up to."

Diamond nods her head, pretending to blow Jasmine off.

CHAPTER 10

"Welcome to our palace," Nathan turns to Pierre and shakes his hand. He stares a Pierre for a while, then continues, "the House of Africology. The place where magic is made by the new wearers of the crown of the Magi."

Pierre looks at the mansion in amazement.

"Although Robert and Mischel aren't back from Egypt yet, I still wanted you to come and break bread with Dr. Thomas, Abraham, and myself. So, I suggested that you didn't bring your wife because it's a brother thing," Nathan shows Pierre that he has a sense of humor.

Abraham and Dr. Thomas both look at Pierre and nod their heads while shaking his hand.

"This way my brother." Nathan leads the way to the sitting room. "Sit anywhere you'd like and get comfortable.

Pierre looks to see if someone else would sit first. Everyone waits for Pierre to take a seat. Then they sit.

"I'm honored that you invited me to your headquarters."

"It is our pleasure," replies Nathan. "So, how are things your way?"

"Things are the same. We're just attempting to recruit without recruiting."

"Membership is always difficult, especially in this day and time. It's difficult to inspire people. Times have changed, but have they?"

"There's nothing new under the sun." Pierre responds, "an interesting biblical verse like our people are destroyed for lack of knowledge."

"I agree. The only thing that has changed is the position of energy and the way it's explained. Somehow, we must get the knowledge to the people without letting them know that it is the sacred knowledge of old. Then we can see what kind of lack is occurring."

Abraham chimes in, "the change of energy is why I advocate for people, especially the youth to get involved with Computer Technology. A lot of the knowledge is here."

"Internet of Things is the major focus right now. The powers that be are investing big money into getting modern things to the internet," adds Dr. Thomas.

Pierre asks, "do you have an idea of how to get the knowledge to the people?"

"Of course, but it will take all of our groups to influence the masses from our different perspectives, so they have an incentive, instead of hearing the threat that your ancestors died for the right," answers Nathan, "we must join for the common good of the people. This is the only way I can see, at this time, for them to get involved."

***

Brother Hill receives an urgent message from Mahogani.

It reads, "come to the empowerment center as soon as possible. We have been hit and have a serious problem."

Brother Hill drives to the empowerment center, not knowing what to expect. When he arrives, the center is surrounded by the police, fire trucks, and ambulances.

Brother Hill jumps out of his vehicle. "What happened?"

Someone in the crowd answers, "all we know is some armed men went in. They say someone is dead."

Brother Hill begins to walk around in circles. He is in disbelief. "What!?" Brother Hill looks around for people who work in the center. He sees no one.

Then he receives a text message, "meet at the auto shop."

Brother Hill walks to the auto shop which is shaped like a two-story pyramid. When he gets there, a secret meeting is being held.

Mahogani is on the screen. We were hit by some masked people with guns. They kidnapped Jasmine and Diamond. We have to get word to The House of Africology.

"Rumor has it out here that one of ours has been killed," questions Brother Hill.

"We will speak on that later. Right now, we need to get some people to locate the two girls. Mischel and Robert haven't been heard from in weeks. So, Brother Hill I need you to get the info to Elder Nathan."

"I'm on it."

***

Nathan, Pierre, Abraham, and Dr. Thomas are enjoying a meal.

"So, I heard y'all got some artists. If you need some studio time let us know. I think the elder wouldn't have a problem with your membership occupying some time at Tama-Re Studios," Abraham brings up.

"Oh yeah?" Pierre states.

"I believe we can give some free studio time."

"I think we can make that happen," adds Nathan. "How much time depends on a number you feel that's important." Nathan looks at Pierre and continues, "what's important?"

"3-5-7 equal 15. Christ consciousness and Saturn. I believe 15 is an important number."

"15 it is. Abraham let's give him 15 hours of free studio time."

"I'm on it elder."

Just then the doorbell rings. A few seconds and Brother Hill dashes in. "Elder Nathan, I need to speak to you."

Nathan in a calm manner says, "excuse me gentlemen. Let me go handle this." Nathan then looks at Brother Hill. He motions with his hand, leading Brother Hill out of the room. Nathan leaves after him.

They walk back towards the door.

Brother Hill impatiently says, "Elder, we've been hit."

"Hold on young brother, what do you mean been hit?"

"Mahogani, says some mask people stormed the center and kidnapped two of our girls. Someone might be dead as well."

"Did she tell you that someone was dead?"

"No, but..."

Nathan stares at Brother Hill, "okay, well go back to the center." Nathan hands a card to Brother Hill. "Once you find out more information, call me at this number." Nathan remains calm. He lets Brother Hill out and returns to where the brothers are eating.

He reenters like nothing is going on. He listens to the conversation. He doesn't say anything. He goes off into a stare as he thinks of the next move.

***

"I was told that Robert and Mischel have been handled," Cue tells the person on the phone.

"Excellent, were their bodies recovered," the unknown voice asks.

"No."

"We have to be cautious then."

"I already turned them back."

"Well, we are going to have to take some drastic measures, then. You may have moved too soon."

The phone hangs up.

"Welcome back home," Cue looks at his two wives.

"I hope we never have to do that again," comments Jazmine.

Diamond includes, "the process was grueling. It was amazing but painful."

"But it's all for the family," reassures Jazmine.

"Your loyalty is well taken," Cue lets them know.

"Our job wasn't done. We didn't see Robert or Mischel."

"They have been taken care of," encourages Cue. "Your bodies went through a serious transformation. The two of you need to rest. So, I'm sending you to Dubai for a few weeks."

"Thank you," Diamond and Jazmine enthusiastically express.

"Are you going with us?" Jazmine asks.

"No, I have some business to handle here."

Diamond and Jazmine look disappointed.

***

When Pierre leaves, Nathan tells Abraham and Dr. Thomas the bad news. "We have several issues. The center will be looked at as unsafe. So, we have to beef up security. This also hits us hard because it will stunt any possibility of us pushing for the 30th Street Corridor project. The mayor will get good momentum from this incident."

"Do you think Cue had something to do with this?" Abraham asks.

"I have little doubt that he's involved, but my question is if Pierre and Cue are in bed together. It came to my attention that they recently met."

Dr. Thomas assures, "let's not get paranoid. Let's be cautious."

Nathan reaffirms, "yes, let's be. Our main focus is to find Robert and Mischel. As we look for them, we will put a lot of attention towards finding the little girls who were taken from our center."

CHAPTER 11

Robert wakes up. He lays staring into the air.

The dwelling Idham Ibn Khalid took Mischel and him to is covered with a glass ceiling.

Eventually, Mischel awakes, "hey love."

"You are amazing," replies Robert.

Mischel smiles.

Robert turns towards Mischel and says, "I was laying here thinking."

"About?"

"I am convinced more than ever that Africa is too dangerous. We, without a doubt, have to bring Africa to Milwaukee instead of taking our people to Africa."

"So, you still want to build the African community on the 30th Street Corridor property."

"Yes, starting with Egypt," remarks Robert.

Mischel nods her head. "When are we going home?"

"When the time is right."

"When is that?"

Robert sarcastically says, "time will tell." He chuckles because he knows this is not what Mischel wants to hear.

She rolls her eyes. "Okay smarty pants." She pauses, then continues, "let's go to the library."

"Good idea!"

They jump out of bed, get dressed, and leave for the library.

***

When they arrive at the library, no one is there. The doors open and a voice says, "Enter."

Mischel and Robert look at each other. At the same time, they shrug their shoulders and walk inside. Robert walks in front of Mischel.

The doors close behind them, as several more doors open. The pathway is leading them to the scroll. They walk directly to the altar where the scroll is laying.

The door slams behind them.

Startled, they look behind them. The glass turns to a smoke color. They can't see outside.

Mischel nervously comments, "I wonder if the beings can see us."

"I don't know," responds Robert.

Just then, a purple mist spews from the scroll. The glass starts changing colors.

Mischel and Robert look at each other, hoping that they didn't do anything wrong.

Spirit beings appear. It's Dr. Freeman, Seshat, and11 beings including the Grand Master Peter.

"Welcome," Dr. Freeman states.

"Thank you," Robert and Mischel respond simultaneously. The last time they saw all the spirits together was during their initiation in Mexico.

Robert looks at Grand Master Peter, "you made it."

"Yes, I did. But the work is not over."

Robert asks, "the work?"

Seshat interrupts, "as it is taught, 'To whom much is given, much will be required.'"

"What is required auntie? We are ready," Mischel says confidently.

Dr. Freeman says, "as we are on a ladder of achievement in the spiritual realm, you should know that humans, unknowingly to most, are on the ladder of achievement in the physical realm. The physical ladder is sacredly marked from the numbers 1 to 22. After the master number 22, only a few will be able to attain the master number 33, going through a spiritual consciousness, developed through experience, which will give them a desire to serve on a higher plane."

Robert questions, "from the individual to the master builder then to a master teacher?"

Grand Master Peter adds, "everyone is somewhere on the ladder. You must learn where they are and interact with them accordingly."

The 13 beings all mysteriously bow their heads.

Mischel and Robert look confused. Nothing was said before they bowed.

Another purple mist comes from the scroll. A sweet smell fills the room, as the glass turns black.

The 13 beings begin vibrating. A strange hum comes from them. After several minutes, they all say, "we are grateful to be in the presents of The Supreme Grand Master of all Grand Masters, Tehuti."

The Supreme Grand Master of all Grand Masters, Tehuti, partially emerges from the scroll. He isn't as large as Robert remembers. In fact, he appears to be a hologram and is very small. All that is showing of Tehuti is from his waist up.

Tehuti nods in acknowledgement, "the creative forces are not pleased. Many humans have lost their way. They are no longer contributing to your world." Tehuti looks directly at Robert and Mischel. "It is up to you to get as many humans, as you can, to work towards contributing to society."

"May I speak, Supreme Grand Master of all Grand Masters, Tehuti?" Robert humbly asks with caution, because he knows the power which Tehuti holds.

"You may..."

"Can you give us a starting point?"

"First, the sacred knowledge which was once concealed from the masses by the priesthood, because it was too high for them to grasp must slowly be revealed. Those who are ready will have an ear to hear. You are to use the ancient method given by us as identical characters for letters and numbers. Today, you call it numerology." Tehuti pauses, then continues,

"You can examine and reexamine the messages we left over human existence. We even left messages in the King James Holy Bible. We also left messages coded in your body. Further, we encoded the knowledge in your DNA."

Robert and Mischel look as if the information is to advance for them.

But Tehuti isn't fazed by their look. He continues, "Your DNA or Deoxyribonucleic Acid can be broken down into sections. Deoxy means God, Ribo means Rabbi or Lord and Master, Nucleic means center, and Acid is a chemical which has the power to destroy like the most intense fire. Now, what I just told you about the DNA, explain in your own words."

Robert looks at Mischel.

Mischel says, "I will give it an attempt Supreme Grand Master of Grand Masters." This is the first time Mischel has seen Tehuti. She has only heard about him through her lessons, and when Robert speaks of his great power.

"Yes, my child."

"Is it God, our lord and master, you are the fire at the center of our being."

Robert adds, "our soul and subconscious mind."

"The two of you are correct. Next, we gave you humans the knowledge of the RNA which is Ribonucleic Acid. We added an 'm' at the beginning. The 'm' represents the messenger. Mischel, would you like to give another answer?"

"Yes, Supreme Grand Master of Grand Masters," Mischel confidently response, since she was right the first time, "this is when a message is being sent by a master messenger or prophet of God to our subconscious mind. In other words, this is how the divine communicates with us."

"You are correct. This should be the method you use in your endeavors. Look for the coded meaning in stories and words. And listen for the messages being sent from within."

Robert states, "We have several youths in our school."

"I have seen. Yet, you must be cautious because some of them are not who they appear to be."

Mischel looks worried.

Robert replies, "I don't understand, Supreme Grand Master of Grand Masters."

"There are some who have been utilizing the arts and sciences for their own gain. They aren't using them for the good of all people."

"The Aaronites."

Grand Master Peter and Dr. Freeman look at Robert, as if, he has learned what they wanted to teach him.

Tehuti continues, "the two of you must protect the people as well as teach those who are found worthy about the sciences."

Robert asks, "how are we to teach the people? Do we make a secret society like those who walked before us did?"

"No, you should make it open to every has an ear to hear. A platform like a church would be a good place. Teach the laws of the universe. Tehuti puts out his hands as the symbols of KA, Khu, Shen, Thet, Dub, Sekhem, Ib, Hepet, Sema, Shut, Djeneh, Sistrum, and the Waas rotate around. "Look closely, these symbols will give you the answer to the functions of your planet."

"Where can we learn more about them, Supreme Grand Master of Grand Masters?" Robert questions.

"The knowledge of them will appear at the right time. For now, prepare yourself for the great journey ahead. You are needed back home." Tehuti disappears back into the scroll.

The 13 beings disappear as the glass turns back transparent.

The librarian knocks on the glass. "What are you doing in here? How did you get in?"

As the door opens, Robert replies, "we don't know, but we are leaving."

Mischel and he exit the room.

Robert with a sincere heart says, "we apologize for the intrusion."

Mischel and Robert hurry out of the library, as the librarian yells, "come back. Who are you? I demand you tell me now! I will call the authorities."

Robert and Mischel don't look back. They head back towards their dwelling. They are moving so fast that they bump into someone.

Robert says without looking at the being, "I'm sorry."

"Robert and Mischel, is that you?"

They look up.

Startled, Mischel replies, "Abraham, what are you doing here?"

"I'm here to get your new attire."

"Attire?"

Robert says nothing. He looks at Abraham suspiciously.

"Yeah, these are way better than the hoodies I made for you. We need you back in Milwaukee. Something terrible has happened."

"What do you mean?"

"Two girls were kidnapped from the school."

Robert looks at Mischel. His face displays a sense of urgency.

"Let's go, now," exclaims Mischel.

Robert says in a low voice, "see, time always tells."

Abraham leads them to a cylinder shape resembling an elevator. They get in, and it shoots them back to Abraham's underground computer lab.

***

Mischel and Robert enter Nathan's office.

"There you are, we've been looking for you. Where have you been?"

Robert answers, "it's a long story. We will explain later. Could you please give us an update on what's going on, elder?"

"Things aren't going well at all. Some masked and arm men kidnapped two of our girls from the school and the mayor is blocking our project."

"Cue"

Nathan responds, "that's what I've been thinking. I know Cue influences the mayor, but I don't know if he'd go so low as to kidnap the children."

"Cue is a very dangerous man, who would do anything to win," explains Robert.

Nathan lowers his head, "well then, he sounds just like Jacob Moletree."

Mischel suggests, "let's go ask Abraham if he has seen anything from his cameras which monitor the city."

"Is he back?"

"Yes, we saw him," responds Mischel.

***

Nathan, Robert, and Mischel enter Abraham's lab.

"We need to look at your camera footage of the day of the kidnapping," Robert informs Abraham.

"I've been looking but haven't seen anything." Abraham turns on the footage.

They see the men leave out with the children. They get into a van. As the van drives off, it mysteriously disappears.

"There's nothing else."

Robert interjects, "show me all of Cue's properties. I want to see the activities going on during the time the van left our school."

Abraham pulls the footage up. They look at all the properties for hours.

Suddenly Robert blurts out, "right there. For some reason the garage door open and closed. This is probably where they are being held."

"What are you thinking, Robert?" Mischel asks.

"Let's leak information that we are back in town." Robert pauses, "no, better yet, you and

I will go to Cue's club and let him know that we are back. If my hunch is correct, he will make some drastic move."

Abraham suggests, "you should try on your new outfits, before you go."

Nathan asks, "new?"

Abraham answers, "it's a long story. I will explain what happened later. Robert and Mischel, here's your attire." Abraham hands them both a package.

Robert and Mischel walk to the bathroom. They open their packages and put on their garbs.

Mischel's garb is blue and gold. A gold star is on her chest. There are 4 stars on each of her forearms. Her blue mask is trimmed in gold.

Robert's garb is green and gold. He has a gold moon and silver cresent on his chest. His mask is green and gold.

They walk back into the room.

Nathan says, "amazing."

Abraham adds, "it fits perfectly. Here are rings for the two of you. Your garbs will fit inside."

"In these little things," Robert asks.

"They will work. First go and put your clothes back on. Then come out. I will give you further instructions from there." Abraham hands them the rings.

Robert and Mischel put the rings on. They go and switch their clothes. They come back out with the garbs in their hands.

Abraham instructs, "now say Pa Temt-Ta and your garbs will enter and exit the rings. Give it a try."

Robert says "Pa Temt-Ta" first. His garb is swallowed by the ring.

Mischel says, "Pa Tempt-Ta." Nothing happens.

Abraham declares, "it's Pa Temt-Ta not Pa Tempt-Ta. Try it again."

Mischel says "Pa Temt-Ta." Her garb is swallowed by her ring.

"Excellent, now say it. The clothes you are wearing will disappear as your new attire is put on. It will be so quick that we won't see the change of clothes occur."

They both do it. And just like Abraham said, their clothes switch faster than the eyes could see.

CHAPTER 12

"They don't even realize that their people are the ones who laid the platform for this system," Bob claims, as George and he wait for Cue to arrive.

"What do you mean?" George asks.

"You don't know?"

"No"

Bob explains, "their people came with Christopher Columbus to set up multiple businesses in this region. Our people called it, the new land, but people were already here. They were living in peace and harmony. Even when our people arrived, we weren't the most powerful. Overtime, we had to force our way into the power positions that they held. We learned their ways, as they helped us learn to read and write, then we flipped their teachings, and began writing a new history, showing us ruling the world."

George replies, "I don't believe it. I think we had to push them hard enough so they would progress. They were savages, outdated. They walked naked like cavemen."

"Oh George, you are naïve. This country wasn't powerful until the end of World War 2.

Yes, we had pockets of centralized businesses. But it took over 400 years for this country to totally dominate the world. We even had to take on their cultures. Like I said, their people came with Columbus."

"Who are these, 'their people,' George disturbed and irritated asks in a sarcastic but cautious manner.

"They were known as the Marrano. They were the business class."

"Marrano, what?"

"Black people had separate groups. They all had their expertise."

"Give me an example please."

Bob feeling disrespected, keeping a calm and emotionless character, looking like a stoic master, he says, "I'll give you an example of what we called, at least, three of their groups. There were the Moors who were like the soldiers on land. Then the Barbary Pirates who ruled the waters. The third were the Marrano, again the business class."

"I don't believe it. They aren't that intelligent. They could never rule or defeat us."

The phone rings.

"Send him in," Bob answers.

Cue enters the room, "gentlemen."

Bob stands and walks to Cue to shake his hand.

George looks at Cue, as if he is disgusted. He doesn't say hello or anything.

After Cue shakes Bob's hand, he focuses on George, "how are you, good sir?"

This forces George to respond, "hey."

Cue chuckles.

"Take a seat, Cue," offers Bob.

"Thank you, sir. I like your office. It has an old school flavor."

Bob's office is dark brown with a hint of dark tan. It has a chandler hanging from the coffered ceiling with glass indentation, and the walls are custom built-in cabinetry filled with trophies.

His L-shaped desk is exceptionally detailed and expertly crafted from rich hued mahogany wood with a black leather top and beautiful carved detailed legs. A lamp sits on the edge of the desk as two computer screens are positioned separately.

Across from the desk are two cushioned chairs with a floral design.

Cue recognizes that Bob's Victorian style office has purposely been fit to give an air of dominance and royalty.

"Thank you, Cue. Let's get straight to business. What's the latest update?"

"Well, the House of Africology's project is stalled. City Hall is still being lobbied to stop the entire project."

"Good," Bob responds, "this may take some time."

Cue continues, "the kidnapping of the two girls went well."

"What do you mean," George asks.

Cue looks at Bob.

"It's all a part of the plan, George," Bob informs him.

"But I wasn't informed. You didn't give me a chance to alert the law enforcement agencies of the kidnapping."

"That's all been handled, George."

George exclaims "But…"

"George, it's all been handled," reassures Bob.

George looks betrayed.

Bob recognizes it.

Unphased by George, Cue continues the update, "so far, Robert and Mischel haven't been located. They were attacked on their honeymoon in Egypt. Once we find their bodies, the House of Africology will be no more."

"Good work, Cue. You're on the right track." Bob hits a buzzer on his desk.

A large, framed man walks in.

Bob asks the man, "could you get us some coffee please?" Bob looks at George, then Cue for their approval.

Both nod in agreement.

***

Cue leaves Bob's office. As he walks out, he sees Mischel and Robert.

George walks out behind Cue.

A black car speeds towards them and screeches to a halt. Several men jump out wearing black, they are holding rifles. They fire towards Cue and George. Then they jump back into the car and speed off.

Things happened so fast that George and Cue couldn't fall to the ground. Cue remains standing as George lays on the ground. Blood is flowing out of his mouth. George gasps for a few breaths of air, then stops breathing.

Bob comes out of the building. "Are you alright, Cue?"

"Yessir."

Bob yells, "someone call the police."

Cue is in a daze. He is staring at Mischel and Robert, like he sees ghosts.

Soon fire and rescue, an ambulance, and the police arrive. The police begin to question Cue, as they tape off the scene.

Cue is soon released. He goes home. He sits rehashing the events.

Ebony walks in, "Chanokh is on the phone for you."

Tell him I'll call him back.

A few hours go by before he recontacts Chanokh. "They're back."

"Who?"

"Robert and his wife."

"Back from their honeymoon."

"Yeah, but you don't understand."

Chanokh asks, "do you want to fill me in?"

"No, I need you to intensify your push to stop The House of Africology's proposal."

Chanokh replies, "I'm doing my best."

"Chanokh, right now, your best isn't good enough. So do better than your best," Cue furiously hangs up the phone.

CHAPTER 13

Mischel and Robert arrive back at the House of Africology. Nathan started playing jazz and soft R&B throughout the house. He knows that the vibration from music has a certain frequency which aligns with the higher universal realms. He knows the music will calm the atmosphere and keep everyone focused.

As Robert and Mischel walk into the house, they are met by Nathan.

"How did things go?" Nathan asks while looking at them. They look like the color left their skin.

Robert replies, "the creative force guided us to the Prospect Building before going to Cue's club."

"The Aaronite's Milwaukee Branch, that's interesting," says Nathan.

"I didn't know that was their building."

Nathan nods.

"As we stood there, Cue walks out. He sees us. Then..."

Mischel quickly interrupts, "a car pulls up. Several men jump out and shoot the guy who came out of the building after him."

"After who, Cue?"

Robert in a calmer voice says, "yeah, I think it was that detective. I think he goes by the name Double G."

"Wait, George Garner." Nathan is surprised to hear this. "He has been involved in a lot of hits over the years for the Aaronites. It was like he was a mafia made man. He was untouchable."

"Cue probably will tell the Aaronites that we did it." This worries Robert, especially because Mischel was with him.

"I doubt it. If anything, the Aaronites made the move. Time will tell us why. Garner had a very bad attitude. I knew him because he was Jacob's partner. Jacob used to tell us stories about him back in the days. He was bad news for us."

Mischel announces, "well, he's gone now."

"Yeah, he's gone, but who will be his replacement. We can't worry about that now. I set up a meeting with Pierre, the Grand Master of the Enlighten Masons and you. I just found out that one of his members is the teacher who informed me about the incident at the center."

Robert suggests, "I think it would be a good idea to invite the teacher with the Grand Master."

"Great minds think alike. He is coming with Pierre."

***

The meeting was set. Now, Robert and Mischel wait for Pierre and his member to arrive.

At approximately 3 P.M., Nathan walks in with the two members of the Enlighten Grand Lodge.

When, Mischel and Robert see the 3 men enter the room, they stand up to greet them.

"This is Grand Master Pierre and I'm sorry sir, what is your name, again?" Nathan asks.

"Brother Hill."

"And brother Hill," Nathan turns to Pierre and Bro. Hill. He continues, "this is Robert and his wife, Mischel."

Pierre responds, "it is an honor to finally meet the two of you. Elder Nathan has told me some good things about you."

Robert moves forward to shake Pierre's hand. "It's our pleasure to meet you as well." Then he shakes Bro. Hill's hand.

Mischel nods her head in agreement and shakes Pierre's and Bro. Hills hand. She doesn't say a word.

"Let's take a seat," Nathan offers. "I wanted Pierre to meet Mischel and you before our recent tragedy. Then I found out that Brother Hill was a member of his order."

"Pierre, let me ask you a question," states Robert.

"By all means, my brother."

"Why did you decide to be a Mason? I have heard so many things about it. At one point, in my life, I was even considering being one."

Mischel, seemingly uninterested, takes out a crystal wrapped in copper wire. She has taken on a new hobby of wrapping the crystals.

"Well, I never truly intended to be a Mason. In fact, I didn't know anything about it. But, I knew that one of my uncles was a Mason. I kept asking him questions. He kept ignoring me. One day, he started talking about it around me. He was claiming it had a long history and that they ruled the world.

I didn't believe him, I thought there was no way black people ruled the world. Then I found out Masons weren't only black and indeed, they once ruled the world.

I began to study and found some interesting facts or may be conspiracies. Things weren't adding up, so I met another Mason. I asked him how I could be a member because I really wanted to know what went on, on the inside, and the rest is history."

"Wow, now that's interesting," exclaims Robert. "Once you joined, did everything add up?"

"What I read was nowhere near what I experienced."

"Interesting," says Robert.

Mischel finally speaks, "what about the ladies?"

"We have the Order of Eastern Stars."

"You mean the ones who are represented by the upside down 5-pointed star, which represents Lucifer."

"Yes ma'am."

"Yeah, naw that's definitely not for me."

"Can I ask you a question?" Pierre inquires.

"Go for it."

"Do you know another name for Lucifer?"

"Satan."

Pierre chuckles, "that's the normal answer. But what I was looking for was the Planet Venus."

"Really?"

"See, when standing on earth measuring Venus' movement. Venus travels around the sun making an inverted 5-pointed star shape every 8 years."

"Can I add something Grand Master?" Bro. Hill asks.

"Sure."

"In numerology, the #5 represents freedom, adventure, and communication whereas the #8 represents karma, infinity, and also God as in divine power. Many people who have the #8 have the power to be business executives."

"Numerology," Robert responds with a smile.

"Yes, this is what I teach for your school."

Nathan says, "numbers are used everywhere. It's used in ancient Priesthoods as well as Masonry. Numerology is my favorite science. I use it in the banking industry all the time."

Bro. Hill asks, "how so?"

"I use it to pick days to do business. I also use it to understand people. I even use it when selecting an investment."

Mischel, thinking about what Bro. Hill said about him teaching numerology at their school, says, "so, Brother Hill please tell us about the two little girls who were kidnapped."

"Diamond and Jasmine, they had a weird friendship. They acted as if they didn't know each other but knew each other at the same time. It didn't make sense."

"Yeah, that's pretty odd for young people," acknowledges Mischel.

"They were both highly intelligent for their ages. They were just too mature. They just gave off a strange vibe."

Pierre chimes in, "do you have any idea where these young ladies are?"

"We have an idea," answers Nathan.

"If you need any assistance, my Grand Lodge will help in any way possible."

"I know where you can help. We need to pressure the mayor to allow us to start building our community on the 30th Street Corridor property."

"I was talking more about getting the young ladies. I have several goons in my ranks," responds Pierre.

Nathan says, "I understand. The House of Africology's special forces are preparing to get the young girls as we speak."

Robert's eyebrow raises as he looks at Mischel.

Nathan continues, "we need to get our community project started. We have plans to recreate an Egyptian city with modern technology at the helm."

Robert adds, "we want to bring Africa to us instead of us having to go to it."

Nathan states, "we can even put a temple, or I should say Grand Lodge free of charge as part of the décor."

"I like how that sounds. What do you suggest elder?"

"We need to start something similar to Chicago's 21 Century V.O.T.E. that was organized by Larry Hoover. It would be a boost to see the Masons lead such a movement, in this case."

"I hear you elder, but Masons aren't supposed to get involved in the election process."

"Aren't supposed to, but what I know of the Masons, they have always been a progressive order."

Pierre nods in agreement.

Nathan further encourages, "this may help the young folks see that black people really do have power in our community."

"I like how you think elder. I will take the idea to my Grand Officers. I already know the affiliation won't touch it. They are lost in the assumed tradition of Masonry."

Robert states, "this move is radical. It will change the fabric of this city."

"I agree," claims Pierre.

CHAPTER 14

"Hey, what's going on?" Nathan asks Robert as he sits in the study.

"Just sitting here researching for a future sermon."

"Sermon?"

"Oh yeah, you don't know. I was visited by the spiritual realm and told to start a church."

Nathan surprised says, "now that's interesting. What holy book are you going to use and how are you going to preach?"

Robert answers, "I'm going to use the King James Bible, and I'm going to teach about Tehuti.

In fact, I was just doing some numerology work on his name." Robert shows Nathan the paper. He wrote:

Te-Hu-Ti

3 stages

Te= 25 or 7

Ti= 29 or 11

Hu is the first word said when the Egyptian deity Atum created humans.

The Luxor temple initiates entered at the age of 7 and left at the age of 47 (11)

"I think you're on to something," states Nathan.

"I also relooked at Genesis 1: 27.

So, God created man in his own image, in the image of God created he him; male and female created he them.

Nathan adds, "the hermaphrodite or Hermes, the African Deity?"

"Right, who we know is Tehuti. But I was looking more at Genesis, which we know equals 33, in this case, meaning a master lesson, and 1:27, which can be an individual on the third completion because $9+9+9 = 27$."

"Or you can add $1+27$ which is 28, even $7+7+7+7$ is 28, which can be the four female or male wise persons because of the mystical number 7. The gender isn't relevant, the wisdom is. There are several different ways to dissect the verse."

"Exactly, this proves that there are many more hidden meanings in the KJV."

"Like Genesis 1:1 to Genesis 2:2, there are 33 verses. Genesis 2:2 speaks on the 7th day of creation. Man, I miss Dr. Freeman. He used to show us so much."

Robert claims, "he still shows me."

Nathan looks bewildered.

"Grand Master Peter and Dr. Freeman have visited me several times in my dream or unconscious state."

"Why do you say unconscious?"

"I've learned that I had to disconnect my conscious reality to enter into a higher state."

***

A knock is at the door. Abraham walks in, "I have this new gadget I want you to checkout Robert."

"A bird?"

"Not only a bird, but a mechanical Ibis. Really, it's a drone. Faith created it from what I told her about Tehuti."

Nathan comments, "is it ready to go now?"

"Yes," replies Abraham.

"Good, Robert, we should use it to see if the girls are at that building."

"Special Forces mission huh?" Robert sarcastically remarks.

"Yep," Nathan responds.

"Abraham, can we launch it to 3254 West Burleigh Street?" Robert inquires.

"Sure thing."

"Elder Nathan, let me ask you a question."

"Go for it."

"Using numerology, would I add up the address number and street name to know the vibration of the establishment?"

"No, just the address number. So, right now, the building is vibrating on some stable but chaotic adventurous collaboration. At other times, it could be a stable and free place to create some type of partnership. It has two poles. The energy moves between the two poles like the ocean tide ebbs and flows each day."

Robert asks, "which day do you think we should launch the Ibis?"

"(3+2+5+4= 14 or 5) any day because the #5 touches all numbers. It just depends on the outcome you want," answers Nathan.

"Well, since we don't know if the girls are there or not. I think we will launch on a #3 day. We may have to get a little creative."

As Robert was explaining his logic. Nathan receives a text message from Pierre.

Nathan reads it aloud. "The Grand Lodge is all in. We are waiting on your next instructions, elder."

"That's big," replies Robert.

"We want to launch the campaign, immediately. If Cue is responsible, the Aaronites have their hands in this. We have to keep them watching the election front. While we make a move to rescue the girls."

***

Abraham leaves the room.

Nathan says, "Robert, I want to get back to this church thing."

"Okay."

"Have you heard of the Crypto-Jews?"

Robert replies, "not that I can remember."

"The Crypto-Jews were the group of Africans who were expelled from Spain in 1492 A.D. with the Moors. They were the business class."

"Why are they known as Crypto-Jews?"

"They moved around a lot, hiding their true practice within the established culture and practices of the time," Nathan explains.

Robert curiously expresses, "let me get a better understanding. If Christianity was being practice, this group of Crypto-Jews would stop showing their Judaic practice to the masses, openly practicing Christianity instead."

"Right, but they didn't practice Judaism like you may think."

"They weren't Hebrew," inquires Robert.

"No, but they did embrace the Hebrew and Judaic practices."

Robert obviously confused asks, "so they weren't the Jews like the ones we know today?"

"No, they were called Hew." Nathan spells the word. "Once the letter 'J' was added to the English alphabet, the 'H' was replaced by the 'J'. Instead of Hew, they were called Jew."

"I need to look further into this."

"As you wrote, Hu is related to the Egyptian Deity Atum. I think it is time to reestablish the Crypto-Jewish practice." Nathan looks at

Robert. "Oh yeah, another name for them is Marrano."

"I like how this sounds." Robert pauses, "several ideas and pictures are circulating in my mind. I think this is the right path."

CHAPTER 15

The Grand Enlighten Lodge puts out a media blast, stating that they will be supporting Tiffany Ellis for the next mayor of Milwaukee, WI.

Soon after, the House of Africology announced that they would be joining in the effort to elect Tiffany Ellis. Slowly other organizations put their names behind her.

Cue worried, makes a phone call, "Brother Pierre, how are you?"

"I'm doing my best. What do I owe this phone call to?"

"I haven't spoken to you in a while. I was just catching up."

"Ah ok, well just pushing for our candidate to win the mayoral seat."

"I see, why are you supporting her?"

"We think that she will be more transparent."

"What do you mean," Cue curiously asks.

"I'm glad you asked," Pierre calmly replies. "We believe she will let our community know, when things are available for us to take advantage of. Where we can possibly build and make our communities better."

Cue responds, "you don't think my guy is doing that?"

Pierre claims, "not at all. You and I both know that he's giving favors to his people. We need the wealth to circulate amongst all of us, not just the few elites."

"I see. I wish you would have come to me first. If you needed something, I believe I could have made some arrangements for you."

Pierre answers, "my brother, I shouldn't have to come to you. It should already be known that several of us have plans. We are the people who want to eat in this city."

"I understand. Is your selection final?"

"Stamped and sealed."

"Well, I wish you luck."

"And I wish you the same luck."

***

The House of Africology received some good intel on what was going on at the building at 3254 West Burleigh Street.

Robert released the Ibis from different locations at different times close to the building, so he wouldn't get spotted at one place.

They even sent packages and food deliveries to the building.

Several armed men were seen at the building. It seemed like they had 3 shifts per day.

A few young ladies were seen carrying groceries into the building, occasionally.

The House of Africology surmise that if the girls weren't in there, there was possibly some type of illegal activity going on.

***

Robert announces that he is starting a church. He sends an invitation to Cue.

Cue comments to Nefer and Ebony, "do you believe this guy. Now, he's a preacher. He just doesn't know what he wants to do."

The ladies don't say anything.

Cue motions his hand for them to leave. Then he calls Chanokh.

Chanokh answers the phone on the third ring. "Yes, may I help you?"

"We have a problem."

"What do you mean?"

"If my hunches are right, the House of Africology is behind the push to oust you. Robert just sent me an invitation to his church's grand opening."

Chanokh chuckles, "oh he's a pastor now. He's joining the ranks of the other thousand. Classic."

Cue says, "that's my point. He's joining the ranks of the others. I know Robert's potential. If he gets in good with the other faith leaders, he can easily sway them to vote for Ellis."

"From that point, yeah we do have a problem." Chanokh is silent. Then he asks, "do you have a plan?"

"I think you will have to announce the approval of the House of Africology's project. When I spoke to Pierre, his main concern was transparency and the growth and development of the black community. With the announcement, the people will see that you are attempting to do something big for them. This move should give us a good number of black voters."

"Should I inform Nathan that their plan has been approved?"

"No, let's use it as a shock factor, just in case my hunch is wrong, and they aren't leading the election of Ellis. If they aren't leading the way, this may cause them to take their support away from Pierre and back you."

"Got it, boss."

They hang up.

***

Cue makes another phone call. "Joe, how are you?"

"I'm well, boss. What's going on?"

"We're going to have to move the packages. It's getting kinda hot."

"I see, no disrespect, but you know we need some more money to make that happen." Joe a tall light complexion, bald head African American man informs Cue. "My guys are starting to wonder what the package is. I can't keep them from not knowing too much longer."

"I understand. Once the move is made, I'm going to need you to eliminate the package."

"That wasn't a part of the plan, and that service is really going to cost."

"I figured. Let's negotiate a price. But for now, I'm going to need you to move the package."

Joe replies, "I'll move it, after we agree upon the price."

"I don't have that much time. I need it moved now," Cue upsettingly replies. Then he calms down. "But I get where you're coming from."

"It's business not personal. I don't want any of my people hurt, killed, or in jail."

"Gotcha, come up with a price and we'll talk."

"I'll hit you back in a few, after I crunch these numbers."

"Okay," Cue hangs up the phone. He is furious. He hates the idea that one of his employees would pressure him for money, especially since he already paid a million dollars for the project.

CHAPTER 16

The same day Tiffany Ellis announced her campaign slogan "My Milwaukee Too!!!" Chanokh released to the media that he was going to make a special announcement.

The media was in place to hear the mayor.

Chanokh walks to the podium with his entrusted colleagues. He looks around, satisfied at the amount of news outlets present. He states, "I'm announcing that we've approved a major project for the 30th Street Corridor area. It involves 19 acres and will be led by The House of Africology. We're hoping that this project will bring a great example of community and many job opportunities. Thank you." Chanokh turns to leave.

Some media personnel yell, "Mr. Mayor, Mr. Mayor."

But Chanokh ignores them, continuing to walk to his office.

***

Mishel and Robert are walking on Lake Michigan, through the ritual labyrinth, when they hear the news. They look at each other. They hug and kiss each other, recognizing the success.

Robert calls Nathan, "you did it again."

"We did it. It's a team thing not an individual thing. But let's not get too happy, until the project is complete. The mayor still has a lot of time in office. This may just be a ploy."

"Got it, I'll talk to you later," Robert gives reverence to Nathan's strategy.

"See you soon."

They hang up the phone.

"Mischel, let's walk to the last sight again. I think I have a better understanding of it."

"Okay."

They walk to the sight. Robert walks around the square before entering the pillars, as Mischel watches.

"Instead of walking it, the normal way, let's go up there." Robert is speaking about the sidewalk closest to the mansions across the street.

They walk to it.

"As we see we have 5 pillars to our right. It's separated by a sidewalk then there are 4 more pillars and 3 pillars in a curved shape. The 3-4-5 is the numbers from the Pythagorean

Theorem." Robert leads Mischel to the middle pillar of the 3 pillars in the curved shape. "Stand here and look down. What do you see?"

"Like you made mention before, it looks like some sort of compass since it has N, E, S, W. So, I'm assuming it's North, East, South, and West."

"Agreed and do you remember what section you're standing in?"

"The southeast," replies Mischel.

"If you look up the hill towards the northwest, what do you see?"

"Looks like an old light tower."

Robert states, "that's sort of off to the side, would you agree?"

"I can agree. So, if that's the case, I see the Ascension sign on the hospital."

"Back in the days, all men of value studied geometry. The first proposition is using two points, labeling the two points A & B, place a compass on each. Then draw a circle for each. Where they overlap, mark that C. Drawing a line between A & B, A & C, and B & C, you will have an equilateral triangle. Do you see something like that?"

"Yes, it's the capital letter 'A' in the center of the circles, which look like they've been drawn using a compass as well."

Robert says, "you are on point. It's the foundation like the compass on the ground here. If you look back at where we started and off to the side, you see the sidewalk looks like the #4. The triangular shape of the grass makes the triangular shape of the #4. The number 4 represents the foundation."

"Wouldn't the triangle represent the 3-4-5 of the Pythagorean Theorem?"

"Bingo."

"This is perfectly laid out," responds Mischel. "It's so obvious if you understand the sciences.

"Even more than that, the three ritual sights represent knowledge, wisdom, and understanding."

"How so?"

"The Royal Star of the Bull sight is the knowledge. It's the open eye. It's like a curious youth. Then the Royal Star of the Man sight is the wisdom because it resembles the key of life, 7 liberal arts and sciences, and the 4 pillars separated into two sets. It's the adulthood. The partnership is based on the needed unity of the adult male and female to create life which is needed, in its natural form, to begin all life."

"So, I'm assuming this, the Royal Star of the Earth is represented by the compass. Since the compass has 4 points, this is the foundation of some type of physical manifestation. But from your sequence explanation, wouldn't old age be wisdom instead of understanding."

Robert asks, "why do you say this is old age?"

"Looking up the hill, the light house sort of reminds me of a cane. So, this is like an old person who needs the help of a cane to lean on."

"Great explanation, well, wisdom doesn't mean one understands how to use the knowledge. It only means one is wise with the information. On the other hand, understanding means one knows how to actively use both the knowledge and wisdom."

"Well, thank you sir."

"My pleasure, my love. Let's wrap it up and go for a ride. I want to drive past that building on Burleigh."

***

Cue answers the phone, "yes may I help you?"

"Cue, buddy, this is Bob."

"I've been waiting for your call, sir."

"Tell me what's going on with the mayor's announcement."

"We ran into a snag. We are going to lose the black vote in the city. So, I made the decision to let the House of Africology have their project. This may give us sometime to win some of the votes back."

"You should have contacted me first. We're not worried about the black votes. We are worried about the city's economy."

Cue replies, "without the black votes, the mayor will lose."

"Black people are gullible. We would have come up with a plan."

Cue feels disrespected. He sits silently as he absorbs what Bob just said, thinking over the next words to say. He knows if he says anything wrong, it will upset Bob. He cautiously says, "I understand. I will let you know next time. I made a mistake. I apologize."

"If you want to keep a working relationship with me, you have to inform me before you make a move that affects what we already agreed upon. Is that understood?"

"Yessir."

"No need to cry over spilled milk. I'll talk to you soon." Bob hangs the phone up without waiting for Cue to respond.

***

Joe and Cue agreed upon a payment. Joe is meeting his crew in front of the building, planning to move the package. As they stand there, several black SUVs with tinted windows pull up.

Several men, all dressed in black, jump out of each SUV and begin shooting at Joe's crew.

The crew takes cover and begins firing back.

An intense gun battle occurs as Robert and Mischel are a half of a block away. They hear the gun battle and exit their car.

Mischel looks at Robert, "this is the best time as any to see if the girls are in the building."

Robert nods in agreement.

They both say, "Pa Temt-Ta." Their suits replace their clothing. Then they run towards the building. The gun battle is so intense that they aren't seen slipping into the building.

As they go in, they are met by several gun men. The men shoot at them as Mischel and Robert jump on separate walls, avoiding being struck by the bullets.

Mischel pulls out her sword, she kills one of the men.

Robert moves close enough to disarm two other men. They are now in a hand-to-hand combat. Robert is struck and knocked to the ground, but quickly jumps back to his feet.

Mischel is still avoiding the other gun men who are firing at her.

Robert is able to grab one of the men, while the other one lunges a knife towards Robert. Robert pulls the man in the direction the other man is thrusting his knife, stabbing the man Robert is holding. The man falls to the ground lifeless. Robert continues to fight the other man whose knife was stuck in the lifeless one. Robert does a sweeping leg takedown, hitting the man perfectly. The man looses his balance and falls to the ground. Robert pulls out his flail, striking the man, ending his life.

He looks towards Mischel and goes after the other gunmen who are shooting at her. They didn't see him coming. Robert uses his Crook to grab one by the neck. The other man turns towards him and shoots, he hits his partner.

Mischel moves close enough to him to fatally strike him with her sword.

"That was a good workout," says Robert.

Mischel laughs, "the girls."

They walk through the building. Finally locating the girls.

"Come with us," Mischel says as Robert and her untie them.

"Stay close to us," Robert commands.

As they exit the building, one of the men from the assault team shoots a rocket launcher towards the building. It's a direct hit. The building explodes into flames.

Joe and his crew lay dead on the ground.

The assault team didn't see Mischel and Robert exit with the girls. The four of them go back towards the car.

Police sirens are heard. The assault team pick up their wounded, jump in their cars, and speed off.

When the police arrive, the only one's left are the men dead on the street.

***

The ride back to The House of Africology is silent.

The girls are extremely nervous. They didn't know what to expect or if they were even safe.

Mischel alerted everyone in the house that they were on the way with the girls.

When they arrived Dr. Thomas, Mrs. Thomas, Abraham, Faith, and Nathan are standing at the door waiting.

As they walk in the house, Faith says, "hi Diamond and Jasmine, we've been looking for you for a while. I'm glad Tehuti and Seshat located you and brought you here."

The girls look at each other. They get extremely more nervous.

Nathan recognizes their body language, "what's wrong? Are you okay?"

"Yessir, but our names aren't Diamond and Jasmine. We are Destiny and Crystal. You may have the wrong people," says Crystal.

Mrs. Thomas rushes to get the pictures of the girls. She passes it around to the others.

Nathan states, "no, we have the right people, but it seems we have the wrong names." He hands the pictures to Destiny and Crystal. "See."

"Yes, this is us, but I don't remember taking these pictures."

Faith suggests, "well, let's get the two of you settled in, get you cleaned up, and get you something to eat." Faith puts her arms around the girls' shoulders and ushers them towards the guest bedroom. While she's walking, she looks back at the others with a bewildered look.

Robert comments, "I wonder what that's all about. Why the name change?"

Mischel also says, "I was wondering the same thing. We need to get to know them better."

"We'll leave it in the hands of the sisterhood to find out," responds Nathan.

Mischel and Mrs. Thomas nod their heads in agreeance.

Forgetting that they were still in their attire, Robert looks down and says, "let's get out of these garbs, Mischel."

They walk to their bedroom and close the door behind them. "Pa Temt-ta!" Their attire is replaced with the clothes they had on earlier.

***

After Robert explains to Nathan what occurred, several hours go by and a news flash about the incident at 3254 W. Burleigh Street hits the airwaves.

The news report was issued by Mayor Chanokh. He gives a briefing of what was found at the scene. "Police are telling us that several deceased bodies were found outside the building, and some charred bodies inside, two appearing to be small children. We will give further information as we find out what happened."

Nathan comments to Robert, "if they claim the two are from our school, we will have to keep the girls with us and make their class much more exclusive."

"I'll attach the school to the church. What do you think?"

"Good idea, we'll send them to one of our branches in another city as well."

***

As the girls eat, Mrs. Thomas and Mischel join Faith and them.

Faith says, "ah Mischel, you're back. I want to introduce you to Destiny and Crystal."

"Hi."

The girls simultaneously say, "hello."

Mrs. Thomas begins the conversation to learn more about the girls. "Tell us a little about yourself."

Crystal starts, "we are twins. Our mother died when we were real young, and we were put in an orphanage."

"We separately went from foster home to foster home. Then we were told that someone had adopted both of us," adds Destiny.

"Yeah, I was driven to a location and that's all I remember," says Crystal.

"Me too," acknowledges Destiny.

"Do you know the name of the person who adopted the two of you?" Mrs. Thomas asks.

"No, all I remember is the drive. Everything from there is blank except for when I saw Crystal next to me in a chair tied up."

"Yeah, that was scary. I was happy to see Destiny, but I had no clue how we got where we were."

Mischel chimes in, after looking at a text message on her cellphone, "we looked the two of you up. There were no police reports about you missing. It's as if you disappeared in thin air."

Destiny says with a shivering voice, "are you going to send us back to foster care?"

Mischel smiles, "I don't think so. I think the sisters and I can come up with a plan for you to stay with us. That's if you want?"

The girls excitingly say, "yes, yes please."

"Let me go talk to the brothers about it, Faith do you want to come with me?" Mischel asks.

"Sure."

Mrs. Thomas stays with the girls while Mischel and Faith go talk with the brothers.

The brothers are in the library, waiting for an update. Mischel and Faith walk in.

"Did the girls talk?" Robert asks.

"Yes, they are twins and orphans whose mother died when they were young. They were separated going from foster home to foster home, when they were informed that they had been adopted together," answers Mischel.

Faith adds, "they both say the last thing they remember was driving to a location. Then they woke up tied next to each other."

Nathan says, "there memories were erased. They don't remember being at our school or anything."

"It doesn't seem like they do," answers Faith.

"Sounds like some real heavy technology was used on them," suggests Abraham.

"Not only that, but they may have been possessed by some other entities because according to Brother Hill, they were fully functional in his class," Robert references.

"Okay, well we aren't going to stress about that now. We will have to see what the mayor's next move is. Then we'll know what Cue and the Aaronites may be up to."

Everyone agrees.

Nathan suspiciously wonders, "but I do wonder if it were the Aaronites who hit Cue's people?"

CHAPTER 17

"I know it was him. Who does he think I am? I'm not Jacob Moletree," Cue sits in his room by himself. He's highly upset. "Who killed my crew and the girls?"

"Hello," answers Bob.

"Bob, did you make the call?"

"Well, Cue how are you doing?"

"I'm not well. I'm trying to figure out who destroyed my property and assaulted my men."

"In this game, sometimes decisions are made without the other person knowing. You should know this Cue. Didn't you just make a decision without letting me know?" Bob reminds Cue.

"Yessir, I get it. No more words need to be said. I stepped out of line. Sorry to have bothered you."

"It's okay. I hope you have your man change his idea on The House of Africology's development plan. But we'll talk soon."

"Got it."

They hang up the phone.

"I'm a black man who knows my history. Hold up, in fact." Cue dials Chanokh, sounding revengeful, "hey, let The House of Africology continue to build."

"Got it boss."

***

A few weeks go by, The House of Africology break ground on the 19 acres located in the 30th Street Corridor.

The building of Africa in the west has begun.

www.ingramcontent.com/pod-product-compliance
Lightning Source LLC
Chambersburg PA
CBHW050402030726
47503CB00006B/1989

* 9 7 8 1 9 5 6 1 7 4 1 9 9 *